Edwin Wiley Fuller

The Angel in the Cloud

Edwin Wiley Fuller

The Angel in the Cloud

ISBN/EAN: 9783337337742

Printed in Europe, USA, Canada, Australia, Japan

Cover: Foto ©Andreas Hilbeck / pixelio.de

More available books at **www.hansebooks.com**

THE

ANGEL IN THE CLOUD.

BY

EDWIN W. FULLER.

Lange, Little & Hillman,
PRINTERS, ELECTROTYPERS AND STEREOTYPERS,
108 to 114 Wooster St., N. Y.

TO THE

HALLOWED MEMORY OF MY FATHER,

WHO,

EVEN WHILE I WAS GAZING UPON THE GOLDEN CITY,

PASSED WITHIN ITS WALLS,

THIS LITTLE VOLUME IS INSCRIBED,

WITH TEARS.

PREFACE.

To those who may favor these pages with perusal, I make this earnest request: that, if they commence, they will read all. Knowing that the best mode of dealing with doubts is to state and refute, successively, I regret that the plan of the present work forces a separation of the statement and refutation. To read one without the other were to defeat the object in view; hence my request.

Many of the subjects of thought are worn smooth with the touch of ages, so that hope for originality is as slender as the bridge of Al Sirat; but in the bulrush ark of self-confidence, pitched with Faith, I commit my first-born to the Nile of public opinion; whether to perish by crocodile critics, or bask in the palace of favor, the Future, alone, must determine. May Pharaoh's daughter find it!

E. W. F.

Louisburg, Jan. 17th, 1871.

PREFACE TO THE SECOND EDITION.

When I offered my Poem to the public, it was with many misgivings as to its reception; knowing full well, that its style was too grave for popular light reading, and its subject-matter too philosophical for the prevalent sensational taste. Yet in a very short time the entire edition was sold, with a steady demand for more.

Public opinion, too, as represented by the Press, was as kind as public patronage; for amidst scores of compliment-ary notices, I can number but three adversely critical. My own State, with unwonted cordiality, welcomed it through every portion of her borders. For these many favors, I take occasion now to offer my sincerest thanks. They inspire the hope, that as I have been met so kindly while bearing only the dull headache of thoughtful reasoning, I will be greeted still more warmly when I offer the flowers of Romance.

Whilst gathering an humble nosegay from the gardens of Fancy, I must bid you, kind readers, a brief *au revoir*.

F.

Angel in the Cloud.

'Twas noon in August, and the sultry heat
Had driven me from sunny balcony
Into the shaded hall, where spacious doors
Stood open wide, and lofty windows held
Their sashes up, to woo the breeze, in vain.
The filmy lace that curtained them was still,
And every silken tassel hung a-plumb.
The maps and unframed pictures o'er the wall
Gave not a rustle; only now and then
Was heard the jingling sound of melting ice, ·
Deep in a massive urn, whose silver sides
With trickling dewbeads ran. The little birds,
Up in their cages, perched with open beaks,
And throbbing throats, upon the swaying rings,
Or plashed the tepid water in their cups
With eager breast. My favorite pointer lay,
With lolling tongue, and rapid panting sides,
Beside my chair, upon the matted floor.
All things spoke heat, oppressive heat intense,
Save swallows twittering up the chimney-flue,

Whose hollow flutterings sounded cool alone.
To find relief I seized my hat and book,
And fled into the park. Along a path
Of smoothest gravel, oval, curving white,
Between two rows of closely-shaven hedge,
I passed towards a latticed summer-house;
A fairy bower, built in Eastern style,
With spires, and balls, and fancy trellis-work,
O'er which was spread the jasmine's leafy net,
To snare the straying winds. Within I fell
Upon a seat of woven cane, and fanned
My streaming face in vain. The very winds
Seemed to have fled, and left alone the heat
To rise from parchèd lawn and scorching fields,
Like trembling incense to the blazing god.
The leaves upon the wan and yellow trees
Hung motionless, as if of rigid steel;
And e'en the feath'ry pendula of spray,
With faintest oscillation, dared not wave.
The withered flowers shed a hot perfume,
That sickened with its fragrance; and the bees
Worked lazily, as if they longed to kick
The yellow burdens from their patient thighs,
And rest beneath the ivy parasols.
The butterflies refrained from aimless flight,
And poised on blooms with gaudy, gasping wings.
The fountain scarcely raised its languid jet
An inch above its tube; the basin deigned
A feeble ripple for its tinkling fall,

And rolled the little waves with noiseless beat
Against the marble side.　The bright-scaled fish
All huddled 'neath the jutting ledge's shade,
Where, burnished like their magnet toy types,
They rose and fell as if inanimate ;
Or, with a restless stroke of tinted fin,
Turned in their places pettishly around;
While, with each move, the tiny whirlpools spun
Like crystal dimples on the water's face.
The sculptured lions crouched upon the edge,
With gaping jaws, and stony, fixèd eyes,
That ever on the pool glared thirstily.
Deep in the park, beneath the trees, were grouped
The deer, their noses lowered to the earth,
To snuff a cooler air ; their slender feet
Impatient stamping at the teasing flies;
While o'er their heads the branching antlers spread,
A mocking skeleton of shade!　A fawn,
Proud of his dappled coat, played here and there,
Regardless of repose ; the silver bell,
That tinkled from a band of broidered silk,
Proclaiming him a petted favorite.
Save him alone, all things in view sought rest,
And wearied Nature seemed to yield the strife,
And smould'ring wait her speedy sacrifice.

The heat grew hotter as I watched its work,
And with its fervor overcome, I rose,
And through the grounds, towards an orchard bent

My faltering steps in full despair of ease.
Down through the lengthened rows of laden trees,
Whose golden-freighted boughs o'erlapped the way,
I hurried till I reached the last confines.
Here stood a gnarlèd veteran, now too old
To bear much fruit, but weaving with its leaves
So dense a shade, the smallest fleck of sun
Could not creep through. Beneath it spread a couch
Of velvet moss, fit for the slumbers of a king.
Here prone I fell, at last amid a scene
That promised refuge from the glaring heat.
Beyond me stretched the orchard's canopy
Of thick, rank foliage, almost drooping down
Upon the green plush carpet underneath.
Close at my feet a crystal spring burst forth,
And rolled its gurgling waters down the glade
Now spreading in a rilling silver sheet
O'er some broad rock, then gath'ring at its base
Into a foamy pool that churned the sand,
And mingling sparks of shining isinglass,
It danced away o'er gleamy, pebbly bed,
Where, midst the grassy nooks and fibrous roots,
The darting minnows played at hide and seek,
Oft fluttering upwards, to the top, to spit
A tiny bubble out, or slyly snap
Th' unwary little insect hov'ring near;
Till, by its tributes widened to a brook,
It poured its limpid waters undefiled
In to the river's dun and dirty waves,—

A type of childhood's guileless purity,
That mingling with the sordid world is lost.

Far in the distance, lofty mountains loomed,
Their blue sides trembling in the sultry haze.
From me to them spread varicultured fields,
That formed a patchwork landscape, which deserved
The pencil of a Rembrandt and his skill;
The hardy yellow stubble smoothly shaved,
With boldness lying 'neath the scorching sun;
The suffering corn, with tasselled heads all bowed,
And twisted arms appealing, raised to Heaven;
The meadows faded by the constant blaze;
The cattle lying in the hedge's shade;
Across the landscape drawn a glitt'ring band,
Where winds the river, like a giant snake,
The ripples flashing like his polished scales.
Above the scene a lonely vulture wheeled,
Turning with every curve from side to side,
As if the fierce rays broiled his dusky wings;
And circling onwards, dwindled to a speck,
And in the distance vanished out of sight!
Complete repose was stamped on everything,
Save where a tireless ant tugged at a crumb,
To drag it o'er th' impeding spires of moss:
And one poor robin, with her breast all pale
And feather-scarce, hopped wearily along
The streamlet's edge, with plaintive clock-like chirp,
And searching, found and bore the curling worm,

Up to the yellow-throated brood o'erhead.
Behind the mountains reared the copper clouds
Of summer skies, that whitened as they rose,
Till bleached to snow, they drifted dreamily,
Like gleaming icebergs, through the blue sublime.
And as they, one by one, sailed far away,
Methought they were as ships from Earth to Heaven,
Thus slowly floating to the Eternal Port.
The Thunder's muttered growl my reverie broke,
And looking toward the West, I saw a storm,
With gloomy wrath, had thrown its dark-blue line
Of breastworks, quiv'ring with each grand discharge
Of its own ordnance, o'er th' horizon's verge.
Some time it stood to gloat upon its prey,
Then, girding up its strength, began its march.
Extending far its black gigantic arms,
It grimly clambered up the tranquil sky;
Till half-way up the arch, its shaggy brows
Scowled down in rage upon the frightened earth;
While through its wind-cleft portals sped the darts,
That brightly hurtled through the sultry air.
And down the mountain-sides the shadow crept,
A dark veil spreading over field and wood,
Thus adding gloom to Nature's awful hush.
The fleecy racks had fled far to the east,
Where sporting safely in the gilding light,
They mocked the angry monster's cumbrous speed.

Then, while I marked its progress, came a train

Of dark and doubting thoughts into my mind,
And bitterly thus my reflections ran:
Strange is the Providence that rules the world,
That sets the Medean course of Nature's laws;
Sometimes adapting law to circumstance,
But oftener making law fulfilled a curse.
You brewing storm in verdant summer comes,
When vegetation spreads its foliage sails,
That, like a full-rigged ship's, are easier torn;
Why comes it not in winter, when the trees,
With canvas reefed by Autumn's furling frosts,
Could toss in nude defiance to the blast?
The murd'rous wind precedes the gentle shower,
And ere the suffering grain has quenched its thirst,
It bows the heavy head, alone of worth,
And from the ripening stalk wrings out the life,
While gayly nod the heads of chaff unharmed.
The rank miasma floats in summer-time,
When man must brave its poisoned breath or starve;
It hovers sickliest over richest fields
While over sterile lands the air is pure;
The tallest oak is by the lightning riven,
The hateful bramble on the ground is spared;
The crop man needs demands his constant work,
The weeds alone spring forth without the plow;
The sweetest flowers wear the sharpest thorns,
The deadliest reptiles lurk in fairest paths!
  Wherever Nature shows her brightest smile,
'Tis but a mask to hide her darkest frown.

The tropics seem an Eden of luscious fruits
And flowers, and groves of loveliest birds, and lakes
That mirror their gay plumage flitting o'er;
Where man may live in luxury of thought,
Without the crime of schemes, or curse of toil—
The tropics seem a Hell, when all with life
Are stifled with the foul sirocco's breath;
When from the green-robed mountain's volcan top,
A fire-fountain spouts its blazing jet
Far up against the starry dome of Heaven;
Returning in its vast umbrella shape,
Leaps in red cataracts adown the slope,
Shaves clean the mountain of its emerald hair,
And leaves it bald with ashes on its head.
Below, the valley is a crimson sea,
Whose glowing billows break to white-hot foam;
And as they surge amid the towering trees,
They, tottering, bow forever to the waves;
'The leaves and branches, crackling into flame,
Leave only clotted cinders floating there;
The darting birds, their gaudy plumage singed,
Fall fluttering in, with little puffs of smoke.
The fleeing beasts are lapped in, bellowing,
And charred to coal, drift idly with the tide.
The red flood, breaking through the vale, rolls on
Its devious way towards the sea; the glare
Illuminating far its winding track,
As if a devil flew with flaming torch,
Or when an earthquake gapes its black-lined jaws,

And, growling, gulps a city's busy throng
Into its greedy bowels. Or the sea bursts forth
Its bands of rock, and laughing at "Thus far!"
Rolls wildly over peopled towns, and homes
In fancied safety; playing fearful pranks,
O'er which to chuckle in its briny bed;
Jeering the stones because they cannot swim,
And crushing like a shell all work of wood;
Docking the laden ships upon the hills,
And tossing lighter craft about like weeds;
Till, wearied with the spoiling, sinks to rest.

'Thus Nature to herself is but half kind,
But over man holds fullest tyranny;
And man, a creature who cannot prevent
His own existence! Why not happy made?
For surely 'twere as easy to create
Man in a state of happiness and good,
And keep him there, as to create at all.
If misery's not deserved before his birth,
Then misery must from purest malice flow;
Yet malice none assign to Providence.
    But some may say: Were man thus happy made,
He would not be a person, but a thing,
And lose the very seed of happiness,
The consciousness of merit. Grant 'tis true!
Then why does merit rarely meet reward?
And why does there appear a tendency,
Throughout the polity divine, to mark

With disapproval all the good in man,
And bless the evil? Through the entire world
Is felt this conflict: some strange power within
Exciting us to good, while all events
Proclaim its folly.   Throughout Nature's laws,
Through man in every station, up to God,
This fatal contradiction glares.   The storm,
With ruthless breath, annihilates the cot
That, frail and humble, shields the widow's head;
And while she reads within the use-worn Book
That none who trusts shall e'er be desolate,
The falling timbers crush the promise out,
And she is dead beneath her ruined home!
The prostrate cottage passed, the very wind
Now howls a rough but fawning lullaby
Around the marble walls, and lofty dome,
That shelter pride and heartless arrogance.

And when the Boaz Winter throws his skirt
Of purest white across the lap of Earth,
And decks her bare arborial hair with gems,
Whose feeblest flash would pale the Koh-i-noor,
The rich, alone, find beauty in the scene,
And, clad in thankless comfort, brave the cold.
The gliding steels flash through the feathery drifts,
The jingling bells proclaiming happiness;
Yet 'neath the furry robe the oath is heard,
And boisterous laughter at the ribald jest.
The coldest hearts beat 'neath the warmest clothes;

And often all the blessings wealth can give,
Are heaped on one, whose daily life reviles
The very name of Him who doth bestow.
While in a freezing garret, o'er the coals
That, bluely flickering with the feeble flame,
Seem cold themselves, a trusting Christian bends;
Her faith all mocked by cruel circumstance.
The cold, bare walls, the chilling air-swept floor;
Some broken stools, a mattress stuffed with straw,
Upholstering the apartment. Through the sash,
The wind, with jaggèd lips of broken glass,
Shrieks in its freezing spite. A cold-blued babe,
With face too thin to hold a dimple's print,
With famished gums tugs at the arid breast,
Thrusting its bare, splotched arms, in eagerness,
From out the poor white blanket's ravelled edge.
Beside the mother sits a little boy,
With one red frost-cracked hand spread out, in vain,
To warm above the faintly-burning coals;
The other pressing hardly 'gainst his teeth
A stale and tasteless loaf of smallest size,
Which lifting often to the mother's view,
He offers part; she only shakes her head,
And sadly smiles upon the gaunt young face.
Yet in her basket, on a pile of work,
An open Bible lies with outstretched leaves,
Whose verses speak in keenest irony:
"Do good," and "verily thou shalt be fed."

And so through all the world, the righteous poor,
The wicked rich.   Deceit, and fraud, and craft
Reap large rewards, while pure integrity
Must gnaw the bone of faith, with here and there
A speck of flesh called consciousness of right,
To reach the marrow in another world.
But man within himself's the greatest paradox ;
"A little animal," as Voltaire says,
And yet a greater wonder than the sun,
Or spangled firmament.   That little one
Can weigh and measure all the wheeling worlds,
But find swithin his "five feet" home, a Sphinx
Whose riddle he can never solve.
                              "Thyself,"
The oracles of old bade men to know,
As if to mock their very impotence ;
And man, to know himself, for centuries
Has toiled and studied deep, in vain.—
Not man in flesh, for blest Hippocrates
Bright trimmed his lamp, and passed it down the line,
And each disciple adding of his oil,
It blazes now above the ghastly corpse,
Till every fibre, every thread-like vein,
Is known familiar as a city's streets ;
The little muscle twitching back the lip,
Rejoicing in a name that spans the page.
But man in mind, that is not seen nor felt,
But only knows he is, through consciousness.
He sees an outside world, with all its throng

Of busy people who care not for him,
And only few that know he does exist;
And yet he feels the independent world
Is but effect produced upon himself,
The Universe is packed within his mind,
His mind within its little house of clay.
What is that mind? Has it a formal shape?
And has it substance, color, weight, or force?
What are the chains that bind it to the flesh?
That never break except in death, though oft
The faculties are sent far out through space?
Where is it placed, in head, or hands, or feet?
And can it have existence without place?
And if a place, it must extension have,
And if extended, it is matter proven.
Poor man! he has but mind to view mind with,
And might as well attempt to see the eye
Without a mirror! True, faint consciousness
Holds up a little glass, wherein he sees
A few vague facts that cannot satisfy.
For these, and their attendant laws, have fought
The mental champions of the world till now;
That each may deck them in his livery,
And claim them as his own discovery.

Hedged in, man does not know that he is paled,
And struggles fiercely 'gainst the boundaries,
And strives to get a glimpse of those far realms
Of thought sublime, where his short wings would sink,

With helpless fluttering, through the vast profound.
Upon the coals of curiosity,
A writhing worm, he's laid; and twists and turns,
To find, in vain, the healing salve of Truth.

But grant that mind exists in fullest play:
How does it work, and what its modes of thought?
Here consciousness may act, and hold to view
A dim outline of powers, contraposed.
In such a conflict, every one may seize
The doctrine suits him best. Hence different creeds—
Desire battling reason, reason will,
And will the weathercock of motive's wind;
Motive the cringing slave of circumstance.
And here Charybdis rises; no control
Has man o'er circumstance, but circumstance
Begets the motive governing the will;
Then how can man be free? Yet some may say,
Man can obey the motive, or can not.
He can, but only when a stronger rules.
That we without a motive never act,
I do declare, though in the face of Reid.
That that is strongest which impels, a child
Might know, although Jouffroy exclaims,
"You're reasoning in a circle." Let us place
An iron fragment 'twixt two magnet-bars,
What one attracts is thereby stronger proved.
Or it may be the really weaker one,
But yet, because of nearness to the steel,

Possess a relatively greater force.
And so of motives, howe'er trivial they,
The one that moves is strongest to the mind.
To illustrate: Suppose I pare a peach;
A friend near by me banteringly asserts
That I can not refrain from eating it.
Two motives now arise—the appetite,
And the desire to prove my self-control.
I hesitate awhile, then laughing say,
"I would not give the peach to prove you wrong."
But as my teeth press on it, pride springs up,
And bids me show that I am not the slave
Of appetite, and far away I hurl
The tinted, fragrant sphere.
      Was not each thought
Spontaneous? Could I control their rise?
How perfectly absurd to talk of choice
Between two motives offered to the mind!
As if the motive was a horse we'd choose
To pull our minds about. There is no choice
Until the motive makes it; then we choose,
Not 'tween the motives, but the acts.
        If, then,
The spring of action is the motive's power,
The motive being far beyond our sway,
Where is our freedom? But a fabled myth!
And man but differs from a star in this,—
The laws of stars are fixed and definite,
And every movement there can be foretold;

Of man, no deed can be foreseen till done.
At most we can but form a general guess
How he will act, at such a time and place.
Even if we knew the motives that would rise,
We could not prophesy unless we knew
Our subject's frame of mind; for differently,
On different minds, same motives often act.
Hence, we can tell the conduct of a friend
More surely than a stranger's, since we know,
By long acquaintance, how his motives work.
But should new motives rise, we cannot tell
Until experience gives us data new.
Thus we will ride beside a friend alone,
And show to him our money without fear,
Because we know the motives—love for us,
Honor, and horror of disgraceful crime—
Are stronger with him than cupidity.
But with a stranger we would feel unsafe;
Nor would we trust our friend, were we alone
Upon an island, wrecked, and without food,
And saw his eye with hunger glare, and heard
The famished motive whispering to him, "Kill!"
If he were free, would we feel slightest fear?
For all his soul would shudder from the deed,
And never motive could impel such crime.

Upon this principle all law is made;
For were man free he could not be controlled,
And all compliance would be his caprice.

But since he is the tyrant-motive's slave,
The law to govern motive only seeks
And builds its sanction on the base of pain,
As motive strongest in the human heart.
It only falls below perfection's height,
Because there are exceptions to the rule;
When hate and passion, lust and greed of gold,
Prove stronger than the fear of distant pain.
And could the law know fully every heart,
And vary sanction, there would be no crime.

But law itself, and the obeying world,
Are proofs against the grosser form of Fate:
That all is preordained, nor can be changed.
All human life is vacillating life;
We make our plans each day, then alter them.
We form resolves one hour that break the next,
And no one dares assert that he will act,
Upon the morrow, in a certain way;
But cries, it all depends on circumstance.
And this is strange, that while we cannot change
Our lives one tittle by our own free will,
We help, each day, to change our neighbor's course;
And he assists the motives changing ours.
For all relations to our fellow-men,
Are powers that form our lives, in spite of us.
But we may change our motives, often do,
By changing place, or circumstance of life,
By hearing, reading, or reflective thought;

Yet are these very things from motives done,
And motives mocking all our vain commands.
One motive made the object of an act,
Another rises subject of the act;
And to the final motive we can never reach.

The world's a self-adjusting, vast machine,
Whose human comparts cannot guide themselves;
And each is but a puppet to the whole,
Yet adds its mite towards its government;
Here, in this motive circle, lies all Fate.
Our fellow-men with motives furnish us,
While we contribute to their motive fund.
The real power, hidden deep within,
Escapes the eye of careless consciousness;
Who proudly tells us we are action's cause.
Upon this error men, mistaken, raise
The edifice of law in all its forms;
That yet performs its varied functions well,
Because it offers motives that restrain,
Till stronger overcome, and crime ensues.
The motive gibbet lifts its warning arms;
The pillory gapes its scolloped lips for necks;
The lash grows stiff with blood and shreds of flesh;
The treadmill yields beneath the wearied feet;
And Sabbath after Sabbath preachers tell
Of judgment, and of awful Hell, and Heaven;
All these, to stronger make, than lust of sin.
And yet, to lead my reasoning to its end,

I find a chaos of absurdity.
If I am by an unruled motive driven,
Why act at all? Why passive not recline
Upon the lap of destiny, and wait her arms?
Why struggle to acquire means of life,
When Fate must fill our mouths or let us die?
Why go not naked forth into the world,
And trust to Fate for clothes? Why spring aside
From falling weight, or flee a burning house,
Or fight with instinct strength the clasp of waves?
Because we cannot help it; every act
Behind it has a motive, whose command
We, willing or unwilling, must obey.

Law governs motives, motives create law;
Between the reflex action man is placed,
The helpless shuttlecock of unjust Fate!
Now passive driven to commit a crime,
Then by the driver laid upon the rack;
A Zeno's slave, compelled by Fate to steal,
And then compelled by Fate to bear the lash!

What gross injustice is the rule of life!
A sentient being made without a will,
And placed a cat's-paw in the hands of Fate,
Who rakes the moral embers for a sin,
That, found, must burn the helpless one alone.
All right and wrong, and whate'er makes man man,
Are gone, and language is half obsolete;

No need of words to tell of moral worth
Existing not, nor e'en conceivable;
No words of blame or commendation, given
According to the intention of a deed;
No words of cheer or comfort, to incite,
For man must act without our useless tongues;
No words of prayer, if Fate supplies our wants;
No words of prayer, if Fate locks up her store;
No words of love, for fondest love were loathed
If fanned by Fate to flame.   No words of hate,
For all forgive a wrong when helpless done;
The buds that bloom upon the desert heart
Lose all their sweetness when they're forced to grow;
All pleasure's marred because it is not earned,
And pain more painful since 'tis undeserved.

Man, falling from his high estate, becomes
A brute with keener sensibilities;
Endowed with mind, upon whose plastic face
Fate writes its batch of lies; poor man believes,
And prates of moral agency, and cants
Of good *he* does, and evil that *he* shuns.
With blind content, he rests in false belief,
And happy thus escapes the mental rack—
The consciousness of what he really is.

And yet why false belief?   The world believes,
And acting, moves in general harmony;
Could harmony from such an error flow?

Would all believe, would not some one.
Have doubted by his works as well as faith?
The veriest skeptic walks the earth to-day,
As if he held the seal of freest will,
And shapes his course, and judges all mankind
By freedom's rule.
    Then may not that be true
Which most believe, and those who doubt profess
In every act; as that which few believe
And to which none conform?
    Two paths I see,
One marked Free-Will, the other Fate. The first,
Extending far as human thought can reach,
Through lovely meads with sweetest flowers, and fruits
Of actions clearly shown as right and wrong,
Because of choice 'twixt the two; of laws
With sanction suiting agents who are free;
Of courts acquitting the insane of crime,
Of crime made crime, alone, when done as crime,
Of judgment passed by public sentiment
On action in the ratio of liberty.
Delightful view; but seek an entrance there—
The towering bars of unruled motive stand
Before the path, and none can overleap.

The field of Fate lies open; nothing bars
Our progress there. A thousand different ways
The path diverges. Every by-path leads
To some foul pit or bottomless abyss.

Along each side are strewed the whitening bones
Of venturous pilgrims, lost amid its snares.
Some broken on the rocks of gross decree,
Who hold an unchanged destiny from birth ;
Who will not take a medicine if sick,
Who cant of " To be, will be," and the time
Unalterably set to each man's life.
Some stranded on the finer form of Fate,
Who say it works by means.   Hence they believe
In using all preventives to disease,
In going boating in a rubber belt,
In placing Franklin rods upon a house,
In preaching, and in praying men repent.
These, when one dies, cry out, " It was his time."
Or if he should recover, " It was not."
Their fate is always ex post facto fate,
And knowing not the future, they abide
The issue of events, and then confirm
Their dogged dogmas.
                          Still another class,
Though fewer far in numbers, perish here.
These are the sophists ; men who deeply dive
Beneath the surface of effect, and trace
Our actions to their source.   They find that man,
Made in the glorious image of his God,
Is not an independent cause, but works
From motive causes out of his control.
They find that every mental act must flow
From outside source, then fearlessly ascend

The chain of being to a height divine,
And dare to fetter the Eternal mind,
And throw their bonds around Omnipotence.
As well a spider in an eagle's nest
Might, from his hidden web among the twigs,
Attempt to throw his little gluey thread
Around the mottled wing, whose muscled strength
Beats hurried vacuums in the ocean's spray,
Or circling upward, parts the thunder-cloud,
And bursts above; and shaking off the mists,
With rigid feathers bright as burnished steel,
Floats proudly through the tranquil air.
                              Which realm
Shall now be mine, Free-Will or Fate? The one
Stands open wide, but all in ruin ends;
The other, fair if once within the pale;
But how to scale the barriers none can tell.
Bah! all is doubt. I'll leave the mystic paths
Where, on each side, are ranged the phantom shapes
Of disputants, alive and dead, who fight,
With foolish zeal, o'er myths intangible;
When each one cries "Eureka!" for his creed.
That scarcely lives a day, then yields its place.
A Roman 'gainst a Roman, Greek to Greek,
A zealous Omar with an Ali paired;
A saintly Pharisee in hot dispute
With Sadducees. Along th' illustrious rows
Of lesser lights, who advocate the creeds
Of their respective masters, we descend

To later days and see Titanic minds
Exert their giant strength to reach the truth,
And, baffled, fall.   Locke, ever elsewhere clear,
Here mystified ; Spinoza's dizzy wing
O'erweighted by his strange "imperium ;"
Hobbes, with his new intrinsic liberty ;
And Belsham's quaint reduction to absurd ;
"Sufficient reason," reared in Leibnitz's strength;
Reid, Collins, Edwards, Tappan, Priestley, Clarke,
All push each other from the door of Truth.

None ever have, nor ever will, on earth,
Reach truth of theory concerning Fate.
It stands as whole from every touch of man
As ocean's broad blue scroll, whose rubber waves
Erase the furrows of the plowing keels.

Then, careless whether man be king or slave,
I'll take his actions, whether free or not,
And trace them to their sources.   Deep the dive,
But, throwing off the buoys of Charity
And Faith, and all the prejudice of life,
I grasp the lead of Doubt, and downward sink
Into the cesspool of the human heart,
To find the fount, that to the surface casts
A thousand bubbles of such varied hues :
The pale white bubble of hypocrisy,
The murky bubble of revenge and hate,
The frail gilt bubble of ambition's hope,

The rainbow bubble of sweet love in youth,
The dull slime bubble of a sensual lust,
The crystal bubble of true charity!

Instead of analyzing every fact
Of moral nature, searching for its source,
I'll name a source most probable, and try
The facts upon it; .if they fit, confirm,
If not, reject.   With Hobbes and Paley then
I join; and here avow that all mankind
Have but one source of action—Love of self—
Yet not self-love as understands the world,
For that's a name for error shown by few;
But natural instinct that impels all men
To give self pleasure, and to save it pain;
For pain and pleasure are Life's only modes—
No neutral state—we suffer, or enjoy;
And every action's linked with one of these.
We cannot act without a consciousness,
A consciousness of pleasure or of pain,
The very automatic workings of our frames
Are pleasures, unmarked from their constancy;
But if impeded, they produce a pain.
This instinct, teaching us to pleasure seek,
And pain avoid, none ever disobey;
For be their conduct what it-may, a crime
Or virtue, greed or pure benevolence,
To find the greatest pleasure is their aim.
Nay, start not, critic, but attend the proofs.

A man exists within himself alone,
Himself, or he would lose identity.
To him the world exists but by effects
Upon himself. His actions toward it then
Bear reference to himself. He cannot act
Without affecting self. His nature's law
Demands that self be dealt with pleasantly.

There is no pain or pleasure in the world,
But as he feels th' reality in self,
Or fancies it by signs in other men.
This fancied pain is never *real* pain,
But yields a *real* reflex. Others' pain
Is never pain to us, unless we know
It does exist. Within a hundred yards
A neighbor dies, in agony intense,
And yet we feel no slightest trace of pain,
Unless informed thereof. 'Tis only when we know,
And therefore are affected, that we feel.

The modes of pain and pleasure are then two,
A real and a fancied one. The first acute,
In ratio of our sensibilities;
The last in ratio of our image-power.
These gifts in different men unequal are,
And hence life's varied phases. One may deem
A real pain far greater than a pain
In fancy formed, from others' sufferings;
He eats alone, and drives the starving off.

Another's fancy paints more vividly,
And he endures keen hunger to supply
The poor with food.   And so of pleasure too,—
And this moves all to shun the greatest pain,
And find the greatest pleasure.
                      Different minds,
And each at different times of life, possess
A different standard of this highest good.
The swaddled infant wails for its own food,
Because its highest pleasure is alone in sense;
The child will from its playmate hide a cake
Until it learns that praise for sharing it
Gives greater pleasure than the sweetened taste;
One boy at school proves insubordinate,
His schoolmates' praise he deems his highest good;
Another studies well, because he values more
A parent's smile.   The murderer with his knife,
The maiden praying in her purity,
The miser dying over hoards of gold,
The widow casting thither her two mites,
A white-veil bending o'er the dying couch,
A stained beauty floating through the waltz,
The preacher's zeal, the gambler's eager zest;
All have one motive, greatest good to self!

The tender stop their ears, and cry aloud:
"What! do you dare assert the gambler seeks
With hellish zeal the faintest shade of good?
That he is holy as the Man of God?"

By no means, yet he seeks his good the same.
Not good as you've been taught to apprehend,
But good, the greatest to his frame of mind.
Do not exclaim that good is always good,
And never differs from itself.   Anon
We'll speak of abstract truths, if such there be.
That good and pleasure are synonymous
At times of action, is most surely plain;
For pleasure's but the consciousness of good,
Or satisfaction of our tendencies.
If all the gambler's soul is bent on gain,
Then at the moment gain is greatest good;
But should you reason with him, and explain
Another life, and make it really seem
To him the best, he straight would change his course.

"But," cries my friend, "the preacher, if he's true,
Must labor, not for self, but others' good;
And in proportion as the self's forgot,
And others cared for, does his conduct rise."

But he can not, if conscious, forget self,
For everything he does is felt within;
But deeds for others' good a pleasure give;
If done in pain to self, the pleasure's more.
To gain the pleasure, self is put to pain,
Just as a vesication brings relief.
If he refused to undergo the pain,
Remorse would double it.

Among his flock
Some one is sick ; to visit him is right,
And done, affords a pleasure. Sweeter far
That pleasure, if he walks through snow and ice,
At duty's call!

Sublime self-sacrifice,
Of which men prate, is nothing more nor less
Than base self-worship. Little pain endured
T' avoid a great; a smaller pleasure lost
To gain a larger!

All the preacher's words,
That burn or die upon the stolid ear,
Are spoken from this motive, good to self.
You stare; but it is true. Why does he preach ?
To save men's souls ?—Why does he try to save ?
Because he loves his fellow-men ?   Not so.
His love for them but to the pleasure adds,
Which duty done confers; but all his work
Must be with reference to himself alone,
Though cunning self the real motive hides,
And leaves his broad philanthropy and love
To claim the merit. Let a score of men,
The blackest sinners, die. He knows it not,
And feels no pang; but if he is informed,
He suffers reflex pain. And if his charge,
Remorseful tortures for unfaithfulness.
And only is the state of souls to him
Of interest, as they are known. When known,

It is a source of pleasure or of pain
Which all his labor is to gain or shun.

" This difference then," says one, " between men's lives;
Some live for present, some for future good.
The sensual care for self on earth alone,
The mystic cares for self beyond the grave."

Both love a present self, in present time.
They differ in their notions of its good.
The stern ascetic, with his shirt of hair,
His bleeding penitential knees, his fasts
To almost death, his soul-exhausting prayers,
Is seeking, cries the world, good after death.
And yet his course of life is that alone
Which could yield pleasure in his state of mind.
He suffers, it is true, but hope of Heaven
Thus rendered sure, as much a present good
Is, as the food that feasts the epicure.
The contemplation of his future home,
Which he is thus securing, is a balm
That heals his stripes, and sweetens all their pain.
The penance blows upon his blood-wealed breast
Are bliss compared to lashes of remorse.
So for the greater good, the hope of Heaven,
He undergoes " the trivial pain of flesh."
The epicure cares not a fig for Heaven,
But finds his greatest good in pleasing sense.
And so the man who gives his wealth away

Is just as selfish as the money-slave
Who grinds out life amid his dusty bags.
They both seek happiness with equal zest:
The one finds pleasure in the many thanks
Of those receiving, or the public's praise,
Or if concealed, in consciousness of right;
The other in the consciousness of wealth.

If all men act from motives just the same,
Where is the right and wrong ?   In the effect ?
The quality of actions must be judged
From their intent, and not their consequence.
If two men matches light for their cigars,
And from one careless dropped, a house is burned,
Is he that dropped it guiltier of crime
Than he whose match went out ?   Most surely no !
Then is the miser blameless, though he turn
The helpless orphan freezing from his door ;
And Dives should not be commended more,
Though all his goods to feed the poor he gives.

How then shall we determine quality
Of actions, when their sources are the same,
And their effects possess no quality ?
Two dead men lie in blood beside the way,
The one shot by a friend, an accident ;
The other murdered for his gold.   'Tis plain
No wrong lies in th' effects, for both are 'like ;
And of the agents, he of accident

Had no intent, and therefore did no wrong.
The other killed to satisfy the self,
A motive founding all the Christian work,
And right if that is right. The wrong
Then lies between the motive and effect,
And must exist in the effecting means.
Yet how within the means is wrong proved wrong ?
Jouffroy would say, because a disregard
Of others' rights; for here he places good,
When classifying Nature's moral facts.
He makes the child first serve flesh self,
Then moral self, and last to others' good
Ascend, and general order. What a myth !
As if man thought of others, save effect
From them upon himself. But order gives
A greater good to self; therefore he joins
His strength to others, creates laws that bind
Himself and them, and produce harmony.
He thus surrenders minor good of self,
To gain a greater. This is all the need
He has of order, though Jouffroy asserts
That order universal is the Good.
Yet still he says that private good of each
Is but a fragment of the absolute,
And that regard for every being's rights
Is binding as the universal law !

Regard for others' rights indeed, when men
Unharmed agree to hang a man for crime !

Not for the crime—that's past; but to prevent
A second crime, which crime alone exists
In apprehensive fancy. Thus for wrong
That's but forethought, they do a real wrong.
To save their rights from harm they fear may come,
They strip a fellow-man of actual right,   -
And highest, right of life; then dare to call
Their action pure, divinely just, and good,
And all the farce of empty names.
                              They make
Of gross injustice individual,
A flimsy justice, for mankind at large,
And cry, Let it be done, though Heaven fall!
As if a whole could differ from its parts,
Or right be made from wrong. Yet some may say
That one is sacrificed for many's good,
Or hung that many may avoid his fate;
And that his crime deserved what he received.

But law must value every man alike,
And cannot save one man, or thousand men,
From future evil, only possible,
By greatest evil to another man,
In its own view of justice. Nor can crime
Meet punishment, at mortal hands, by right,
For murder's murder, done by one or twelve,
And legal murder's done in colder blood,
Whose stains are chalked by vain authority.
Authority! the child of numbers and self-love!

Regard for rights of things, indeed, when beasts
And birds must yield their right of life that man
May please his right of taste.   When, during Lent,
The holy-days of fasting and of prayer,
The scaly victims crowd the Bishop's board,
Their flesh unfleshed by Conscience' pliant rule,
Our palates must be for a moment pleased,
Though costing something agonies of death;
And worse than robbers, what we cannot give,
We dare to take.
                    They have no souls, say you?
Nor after death exist?
                    That nothing's lost,
Philosophy maintains as axiom truth.
An object disappears, but somewhere lives
In other form.   The water-pool to mist
Is changed, the powder into flame and smoke.
My pointer dies, his body, decomposed,
The air, the soil, and vegetation feeds;
Yet still exists, although disintegrate.
For there was something, while the pointer lived,
That was not body, but that governed it,
A spirit, essence, call it what you will,
A something seen but through phenomena,
And by them proved most clearly to exist.
A something, not the feet that made them run,
A something, not the eyes, but knew they saw,
A something, without which the eyes could see
As much as glasses can without the eye,

The something "Carlo" named, that knew the name.
The pointer dies, and we dissect the flesh.
All there, none missing, to the tiniest nerve;
Yet something's gone, the more important part,
And can you say that it has ceased to be,
When th' flesh, inferior to it, still exists?
The spirit, if existent, must be whole,
Nor can be parted till material proven.
That Carlo lives, seems plain as I shall live:
He lived for self, and so did I; we fare
Alike in after-life, we differ here
In consciousness of immortality.
But I digress.

        Where is the right and wrong?
This is the Gordian knot no sword can cut,
All sages of the world, with wisdom-teeth,
Have gnawed this file without the least effect.
The thousand savants of old Greece and Rome
Proclaimed a thousand theories of good,
That each, successive, proud devoid of truth.
A myriad moderns have advanced their views,
Each gained a few disciples, who avowed their truth,
And each, by some one else, been proven wrong.
A Bentham marches out utility,
A moral test from benefit or harm.
As if the good depended on effect,
And good would not be good, though universe
In all its phases found no use! And Price
Parades his "reason," with its simple good;

Who'd rather give the question up, than err,
And so declares it cannot be defined.
Then Wollaston declares that good is truth,
Which no one doubts, far as it goes; it goes
Toward good, as far as truth, its attribute;
Beyond, it cannot reach.   And Montesquieu
And Clarke, relation's order preach; a rule
That makes the growing grain, or falling shower,
A moral agent, capable of good.
Then Wolf and Malebranche perfection see,
And therefore good, in God; but their sight fails,
And God may mirror good, but man's weak eyes
Ne'er see it.   Adam Smith, with " sentiment "
Proceeds to dress a thought, and call it, good;
And makes the abstract of a Universe
Arise from puling human sympathy.
The largest concourse follow Hutcheson,
Although the greater part ne'er heard of him.
The world at large believes in moral sense;
They call it conscience!   Oh the precious word!
Though stretched and warped, they almost deify,
And term it man's tribunal in his breast,
Where he may judge his actions, right or wrong.
What nonsense!   Conscience is but consciousness
Of soul, and idea of its good.   We form
This idea from regard of fellow-men,
Association, and from thought.   We find
Sometimes the good of soul conflicts with flesh,
And when we know the soul above the flesh,

We yield to that the preference.   Hence arise
The foolish notions of self disregard.
The savage does not know he has a soul,
And therefore has no conscience.   He can steal
Without remorse.   But when he learns of soul,
He finds it has a good, and by this test
Tries moral actions, are they good for soul?
And this is conscience.

                Yet is conscience changed
By circumstance.   The Hindoo mother tears
The helpless infant from her trickling breast,
To feed the crocodile, and save her soul;
She's happier in its conscience-murdered wail
Than in its gleeful prattle on her knee.
And daily we see one commit a deed
Without a pang, another dare not do.
If conscience may be warped but one degree
By plain Sorites, it may be reversed,
And only prove an interested thought.

To abstract good no man has found the key,
Though in the various forms of concrete good
We see the similars, and from these frame
A good that serves the purposes of life.
We pass it as we do the concept, "Man,"
But never ope to count the attributes.
Our purest right is but approximate
To this vague abstract idea, how obtained,
We know not.   Plato says 'tis memory

Of previous life. Perhaps! 'Tis very dim
In this; and yet it rocks the cradle world
As strongly as the baby man can bear.
And so of truth, or aught abstract, we know
Of such existence somewhere, that is all.
"But we," cries one, "do hold some abstract truth,
In perfect form. The truth of science' laws,
The truths of numbers, each are perfect truths."
The truths of science are hypotheses,
And only true as far as they explain.
But perfect truth must save all facts,
That ever rose or possibly can rise.
"The priest of Nature" thought he held the truth
When throughout space he tracked the motes of light,
And ground the sunbeams into dazzling dust.
Our quivering waves through subtle ether flash,
And drown Sir Isaac's atoms in a flood
Of glorious truth; till some new fact shall rise
To give our truth the lie, and cause a change
Of theory.
          Our numbers no truth have,
Or but a shadow, cast on Earth by truth
Existent in some unknown world. We make
Our little numbers fit the shadow's line
As best they can, and boast eternal truth!
Yet take a simple form of numbers, "two,"
We cannot have a perfect thought of this,
Because the mind directly asks, two what?
'Tis not enough chameleon to feed·

On empty air. Two units, we reply.
Then what is meant by unity?   An " One,"—
The mind can only cognize o-n-e,
Which makes three units and not one.
                               The mind
Must have a concrete object to adjust
The abstract on, before it comprehends.
But two concretes are never two, because
They never can be proved exactly 'like.
To illustrate : suppose two ivory balls,
Of finest mould, and equal weight, precise
As hair-hung scales, arranged most delicate,
Can prove ; yet they can not be shown
To differ, not the trillionth of a grain ;
Or if they could, they may in density
Be unlike ; then to equal weight, one must
Be larger by the trillionth of an inch.
Even if alike in density and weight,
No one will dare assert that they possess
A perfect similarity in all.
The abstract two is twice as much as one,
But our two balls unlike, perforce must be
Greater or less than two of either one ;
But two of one, the same can never be
On poor, imperfect Earth.   Thus all our twos
Fall, in some measure, short of concept two.
And if we paint the concept to the eye,
The figure 2 of finest stereotype,
Beneath the microscope imperfect shows.

And so our perfect numbers, wisdom's boast,
Are faint, uncertain shadows in the mind,
That we can never picture to the eye,
Nor truthfully apply to anything.
We use a ragged, ill-drawn substitute,
That answers all the purposes of life.
The truths of mathematics, so sublime,
Are never true to us, concretely known;
And in the abstract so concealed are they,
No man can swear he has their perfect form.
We can't conceive a line without some breadth—
The perfect line possesses length alone;
Earth never saw a pure right-angle drawn,
Pythag'ras cannot prove his theorem,
The finest quadrant is but nearest truth,
The closest measures but approximate,
And all from Sanconiathon to Pierce,
With grandest soaring into Number's realms,
Have only fluttered feebly o'er the ground,
Their heaven-strong wings by feebling matter tied.

Man is a pris'ner, but the prison walls
Are very vast; so vast the universe
Lies, like a mote, within their mighty scope.
Most are content to grovel on the earth,
Some rise a little way, and sink again;
And some, on noble wing, soar to the bounds,
And eager beat the bars. Beyond these walls
The abstract lies, and oft the straggling rays,

Through crevices and chinks, stray to our jail;
And these we fondly hug as truth.
                                  Poor man!
The glimpses of the great Beyond have roused,
For centuries, his curious soul to flight.
With eagle eye fixed on the distant goal,
He cleaves his way, till dashed against the walls;
Some fall with bruisèd wing again to Earth,
And some cling bravely there, so eager they
To reach the untouched prize, and so intent
Their gaze upon its light, they notice not
The bounds, till Hamilton, with wary eye,
Discovers the Eternal bounding line,
And sadly shows its hopeless fixity.

But man on Earth I love to ridicule,
A little clod of sordid selfishness!
I'll take his mental acts of every kind
And see how self originates them all;
I'll follow Stewart, since he classifies
With shrewd discretion, though his reasoning err.
He places first the appetites; and these
Perforce are selfish, as our self alone
Must feel and suffer with our wants. Our food
Tastes good alone to us. The richest feast,
In others' mouths, could never satisfy
Our appetite for food; self must be fed.
Desires are next; and that of knowledge, first,
Is proven selfish, by his quoted line

From Cicero—that " knowledge is the food
Of mind"—and food is ever sought for self.
Desire of social intercourse with men,
From thought that it will better self, proceeds.
Man's state is friendly, not a state of war,
For instinct teaches him society
Will offer many benefits to self;
And only when he has a cause to fear
That self will suffer, does he learn to war.
Desire to gain esteem, is self in search
Of approbation; like the appetite,
The end pursued affects alone the self.
And lastly Stewart boasts posthumous fame,
When self, as sacrificed, can seek no good.
To prove the motive is a selfish good,
I'll not assert enjoyment after life,
But say, the pleasure of the millions' praise,
Anticipated in the present thought,
And intense consciousness of heroism,
Far more than compensates the pangs of death.
A Curtius leaping down the dread abyss,
Enjoys his fame enough, before he strikes,
To pay for every pain of mangling death.
Affections next adorn the moral page.
At that of kindred, mothers cry aloud :
" For shame! for shame! do you pretend to say
I love my child with any thought of self?
When I would lay my arm upon the block,
And have it severed for his slightest good !"

I'll square your love by Reason's rigid rule,
And test its source.   Why do you love him so?
For benefit he has conferred, or may?
No, as the helpless babe, demanding care,
You love him most.   Your love is instinct then,
And like the cow her calf, you love your child;
That you may care for him, before self moves.
Then do you love him always just the same,
When rude and bad as when obedient?
But I'll dissect your love, and take away
Each part affecting self; and see what's left.
He now has grown beyond your instinct love;
You love him, first, because he is your son,
And you would suffer blame, if you did not;
You love him, too, because he does reflect
A credit on yourself.   You feel assured
That others thinking well of him, think well
Of you.   Because it flatters all your pride
To think so fine a life is part of yours;
Because his high opinion of your worth
Evokes a meet return; because you look
Into the future, and see honors bright
Awaiting you through him; because you feel
The world is praising you for loving him,
And would condemn you, did you not.   And last,
You feel the pleasure deep of self-esteem,
Because you fill the public's and your own
Romantic ideas of a mother's love.

Let each component part be now destroyed,
And see if still you love him. As a man,
He plunges into vice of vilest kinds ;
His bright reflections on yourself are gone,
And people think the worse of you, for him ;
You never smile, but frown, upon him now,
But still you love him dearly ! To his vice
He adds a crime, a foul and blasting crime ;
Your pride is gone, you feel a bitter shame,
A score of opposites to love creep in ;
A righteous anger at his foolish sins,
A just contempt for nature, weak as his ;
But yet you love him fondly, for the world
Is lauding you for " mother's holy love ;"
And you delight its clinging strength to show,
You gain in public credit by your woes,
And get the soothing martyr's sympathy.
But let him still grow worse, and sink so low,
That people say you are disgraced through him,
Your warmest friends will not acquaintance own,
Your love for such an object's ridiculed,
And gains respect from none. Your only chance
Is to disown him. How you loud proclaim,
"He's not my child but by the accident
Of birth !"
              Do yet you love him in your heart ?
This then because you think yourself so good,
So heaven-like, for loving him disgraced,
You go to see him in the shameful jail ;

He spits upon, and beats you from his cell,
And tells you that he hates your very name.
Now all your love is gone, except the glow
Of pity for him chained to dungeon floor;
But he's released, and deeper goes in crime;
Then, lastly, Pity yields. Your heart is stone!

But love was only touched in selfish part,
Yet should you still deny your love is self's;
Of several children, do you not love most
The one whose conduct pleases most yourself?
But love, unselfish, never could be moved
By anything affecting self alone.

The throbbing hearts of lovers beat for self,
And this I'll prove, though Pyramus may vow
He has no thought but Thisbe.
                   Take away
Love's sensual part, which is an appetite,
And therefore selfish, by its Nature's law;
And what remains is, first, a slight conceit
At our discernment in the choice we've made,
And then a pride that we have won the prize;
A pride, that some one thinks we are the best;
A pleasure in her presence, too, we feel,
Because in every look she manifests
Her preference for us. This is flattering
Beyond all else that we have ever known.
A friend may raise our self-esteem, indeed,

By showing constantly his own esteem,
But never can man's vanity receive
A higher tribute than a woman's love!
This tribute, we, of course, reciprocate,
And when together, we increase self-love
By mutual words expressing our regard.
Yet when our love is deepest, if we find
Our Self is not so worshipped as we thought,
Our love grows cold; and when we are not loved
We cease to love.   To illustrate permit:

You're on the topmost wave of fervid love—
A wilder flame than poets ever sung;
You've passed the timid declaration's bounds,
And revel in a full assured return.
There is no need for check upon your heart,
It has full leave to pour its gushing tide
Of feeling forth, and meet responsive floods.
You meet her in the parlor's solitude,
No meddling eye to watch the sacred scene.
The purple curtains hang their corded folds
Before the tell-tale windows; closed the door,
And sealed with softest list.   The rich divan
Is drawn before the ruddy grate that glows
With red between the bars, and blue above.
You sit beside The Angel of your dreams,
And gaze in adoration.   What a form!
Revealed in faultless symmetry by robes
Of rare, exquisite elegance, and taste,

That fit the tap'ring waist and arching neck.
And how superbly flow the torrents of her hair!
Which she has shaken loose, because "it's you ; "
Her great brown eyes that gaze so dreamily
Upon the flowers of the vellum-screen
That wards the fire from her tinted cheek!
One hollow foot, in dainty, bronze bootee,
Tapping the tufted lion on the rug ;
A snowy hand with blazing solitaire—
The pledge of your betrothal—nestling soft
Within your own.
   And thus you sit, and breathe
With tones so soft, because the ear's so near,
The mutual confidence of little cares;
And how you longed for months to tell your love,
But feared a cold rebuke ; and how you dared
To hope through all the gloom ; and how you
   grieved
At every favor shown to other men ;
How now the clouds have flown away,
And all is brightness, joy, and tender love.
Then drawing nearer, round the slender waist
You pass an arm ; and nestling cheek to cheek,
Palm throbbing palm, you hush all useless words,
And thought meets thought, in silent love.
And now and then, you leave the cheek, to kiss
The coral lips; yet not with transient touch,
But with a fervid, lingering pressure there,
As if you longed to force the lips apart,

And drink the soul; while both her melting orbs
Are drooped beneath your burning inch-near eyes.

The parting hour must come. The good-night said,
You rise to leave; and turning, at the door,
You see her head drooped on the sofa's arm,
You fancy she is sighing that you 're gone;
And stealing back on tiptoe, gently raise
The beauteous face, and take it 'twixt your palms;
And gazing on the features radiant,
Distorted queerly by your pressing hands,
You feel that life, the parting cannot bear,
That you must stay forever there, or die!
Another effort, one more nectar sip,
You rush from out the room, and slam the door.
Just on the steps, you meet your rival's face.
He has an easy confidence, and walks
Into the house, as if it were his own.
Poor fellow! how you really pity him!
You can afford to be magnanimous,
And deprecate his certain, cruel fate.
You murmur: " Well, he brings it on himself,"
And turn to go. The window's near the ground,
And slightly raised. Although you know it 's mean,
You cannot now resist, but creep up near,
And with a finger part the curtain's fringe.
You see your darling run across the room
With both extended hands, and hear her say:
"Oh Fred! I am so very glad you 've come,

I feared that stupid thing would never leave,
I had to let him take my hand awhile,
And mumble over it, to get him off."

You grasp the iron railing for support,
And, faint and dizzy with the agony
Of love's departure, cling till all has fled;
Then stagger home without a trace of love.
Yet only Self is touched; her beauty's there,
Her sparkling wit, and her intelligence.
Her manner even, towards you, has not changed,
And, were you with her, she would be the same.
Love's every motive disappeared with Self,
No pride of conquest, no romance of thought;
You meet no sympathy, but ridicule!

A mother's love may last through injury,
Because it reaps the self's reward of praise
For constancy, through wrong. The lover's flame,
Unless supplied with fuel-self, dies out,
For, burning, 't would deserve. supreme contempt.

The less affairs of life are traced to Self.
The code of Etiquette, that Chesterfield
Defines " Benevolence in little things,"
Is but a scheme to give Self consciousness
Of excellence in breeding, and to keep
" Our Circle" sep'rate by its shibboleth.
The stately bow, the graceful sip of wine,

The useless little finger's dainty crook
In lifting up the fragile Sevres cup,
The holding of the hat in morning calls,
The touch of it when passing through the streets,
The drawing of a glove, the use of cane—
Our every act is coupled with the thought
How well Self does all this.

                    Our very words
Are used to gratify the self.   Men talk
By preference, for they judge their words ·
Will gain them more applause than listening.
But if attention yields more fruit to Self,
How patiently they hear the longest tale,
And laugh in glee at its insipid close!
If with superiors, we attend, because
Attention pleases more with them than words;
But if inferiors, we must talk the most,
Since their attention flatters us so much.
The cause of converse, Self, is oftenest food.
How few the talks that are not spiced with " I,"
What " I " can do, or did or will!

                     Sometimes,
The Self is held, on purpose, up for jest;
As when men tell a joke upon themselves.
But here the shame of conduct or mishap
Is more than balanced by the hearty laugh,
Which gives its pleasant witness to our wit.
We never tell what will present ourselves

In such an aspect laughter cannot heal ;
Although it compliments our telling powers.

Attentions to the fair, but seek for Self
Their smiles of favor.   Little deeds of love
To those around us, look for their reward.
The youth polite, who gives his chair to Age,
"Without a thought of Self," is yet provoked,
If Age do not evince, by nod or smile,
His obligation to that unthought Self.

The very qualities we call innate,
Arise and rule through Self.   Our reverence,
Or tendency to worship, is to gain
A good.   Religion grows this tendency
Into the various Churches, all whose ends
Are to secure eternal good for Self.
And those who preach that man does sacrifice
Himself for fellow-men, I ask, why none
Will give his soul for others' ?   Many give
The paltry life on Earth for others' good;
The very stones would cry "O ! fool !" to him
Who'd yield his soul ; for that is highest Self,
And nothing e'er can compensate its loss.

In all these things, Self stands behind the scenes,
And men see not the force that moves them on.
But in the boudoir, 'tis enthroned supreme,
And does not care to hide the cloven foot.

In every home, the marble and the log,
In mammoth trunks, and chests of simple pine,
In rosewood cases, and the pasteboard box,
Are crammed the slaves of Self, to poor and rich,
The clothes that, fine or common, feed its pride.
The velvets, satins, silken *robes de flamme*,
The worsted, calico, and homespun stripe;
The Guipure, Valenciennes, and Appliqué,
The gimp, galloon, and shallow bias frill;
The Talmas, Arabs, basques and palctots,
The coarse plaid shawl, the hood, and woollen
        scarf;
The chignons, chatelaines, and plaited braids,
The beaded net, and tight-screwed knot of hair;·
The dazzling jewels, ranged in season sets,
The pinchbeck, gilt, and waxen trinketry;
The tinted boots, half-way the silken hose,
The shoes that tie o'er cotton blue-and-white;
The corset laced to hasten ready Death,
The leather belt, that cuts the broad, thick waist;
The bosom heaving only waves of wire,
The bosom, cotton stuffed, beyond all shape;
The belladonna sparkling in the eye,
The finger tip, and water without soap;
The rouge and carmine for the city cheeks,
The berries' ruddy juice for rural ones;
The pearly powder, with its poisoned dust,
The cup of flour to ghastlify the face;—
All these, and thousand fixtures none can count,

Man's vanity, and woman's love of show,
Appropriate for Self.
                    And such is Man!
The puzzle of the Universe! Within,
A giant to himself; without, a babe.
A giant that we cannot but despise,
A babe we must admire for his power.
His mind, Promethean spark divine, can pierce
The shadowy Past, and gaze in rapturous awe
Upon the birth of worlds, that from the Mind
Eternal spring to blazing entities,
And whirl their radiant orbs through cooling space;
Or place the earth beneath its curious ken,
And with an " Open Sesame! " descend
Into its rocky chambers, there unfold
The stone archives, and read their graven truths—
Earth's history written by itself therein—
How age by age, a globe of liquid fire,
It dimmer grew, and dark and stiff,
And drying, took a rough, uneven face;
Above the wave, the mountain's smoking top
Appeared, beneath it gaped the valley's gorge;
But smoking still, it stood a gloomy globe,
Naked and without life. And how the trees
And herbs their robes of foliage brought; their form
And life adapted to their heated bed.
And how a stream of animation poured
Upon its face, when ready to sustain;
Great beasts who trod the cindered soil unscathed,

And tramped the fervid plains with unscorched soles.
Great fish whose hardened fins hot waters churned
That steamed at every stroke.   How periods passed,
And fields and forests teemed with gentler life,
The waters wound in rivers to the sea,
Then spread their vap'ry wings and fled to land.
The oceans tossed in bondage patiently ;
Volcanic mountains closed their festering mouths,
And Earth made ready for her master, Man.

It traces Man, expelled from Paradise,
Along the winding track of centuries.
It marks his slow development, from two,
To families, and tribes, and nations vast.
It gazes on the wondrous scenes of war,
And peace, and battle plain, and civic game ;
And lives through each, with all of real life,
Except the body's presence there.   It turns
From man to beasts and birds, and careless strokes
The lion's mane, the humbird's scarlet throat.
It tracks the mammoth to his jungle home,
Or creeps within the infusoria's cell.
It measures Earth from pole to pole, or weighs
The bit of brass, that lights the battery spark.
Is Earth too small, it plumes its flight through
          space ;
From world to world, as bird from twig to twig,
It flies, and furls its wing upon their discs,
To tell their weight, and giant size, or breathe

Their very air to find its gaseous parts.
Now bathing in pale Saturn's misty rings,
Or chasing all the moons of Jupiter
Behind his darkened cone.   The glorious sun,
With dazzling vapor robe, and seas of fire,
Whose cyclones dart the forkèd flames far out,
To lap so hungrily amid the stars,
Is but its playhouse, where it rides the storms,
That sweep vast trenches through the surging fire,
In which the little Earth could roll unseen ;
Or bolder still, beyond our system's bounds,
It soars amid the wilderness of worlds ;
Finds one condemned to meet a doom of fire,
And makes its very flames inscribe their names,
In dusky lines, upon the spectroscope.
With shuddering thought to see a world consumed,
The fate prepared for ours, it lingers there
Until the lurid conflagration dies.
And then seeks Earth, and leaves the laggard, Light,
To plod its journey vast.
                              The smallest mote
Of dust that settles on an insect's wing,
It can dissect to atoms ultimate.
With these, too small for sight, may Fancy deal,
And revel in her Lilliputian realm.
These atoms forming all, by Boscovitch
Are proved, in everything, to be alike ;
And ultimate, since indivisible.
Each in its place maintained by innate force,

And relatively far from each, as Earth
From Sun.

        Suppose, then, each to be a world,
Peopled with busy life, a human flood,
As earnest in their little plans as we,
As grand in their opinion of themselves!
Oh! what a depth of contrast for the mind!
The finest grain of sand, upon the beach,
Has in its form a million perfect worlds!
Or take the other scale, suppose the Earth,
Our great and glorious Earth, to only form
The millionth atom of some grain of sand,
That shines unnoticed on an ocean's shore,
Whose waves wash o'er our whirling stars and sun
Too insignificant to feel their surge.
Another step on either side, and mind,
In flesh, shrinks from the giant grasp.
Yet noble are its pinions, strong their flight;
Thrice, only, do they droop their baffled strength,
Before the Future, Infinite, Abstract!
The first is locked, the second out of reach,
The third a maze that none can penetrate.
The first, alone to inspiration opes;
The second dashed to Earth her boldest wing,
Spinoza's, who essayed the idea God,
And grappling bravely with the grand concept,
So far above the utmost strength of Man,
Placed God's existence in extent and thought;
And filled all space with God. The Universe,

A bud or bloom of the Eternal Mind,
That opens like a flower into this form,
And may retract Creation in Itself!
Alas! that effort so sublime should end
In mystery and doubt.
          .   A Universe,
How vast so ever, has its bounds somewhere,
But Space possesses none, and God in Space,
Would be so far beyond Creation's speck,
He scarce would know it did exist. That part
Of Mind, expressed in matter, would be lost
Amid the Infinite domains of thought.

Yet Man in flesh, the casket of the mind,
Whose wondrous power I've told, is ever chained,
A grovelling worm, to Earth, and never leaves
The sod where he must lie. No time is his
But present; not a mem'ry of the past.
His very food, while in his mouth, alone,
Tastes good. He stands a dummy in the world,
That only acts when acted on. How great
The mystery of union 'tween the two!
A feather touches not the body, but the mind
Perceives it; yet the mind may live through scenes
The body never knew, nor can. Yet not
With vivid life—the sense is lacking there.
The memory of a banquet may be plain,
So that the daintiest dish could be described,
As well as if the eye and tongue were there;

The eye and tongue, alone the present know,
And find no good in anything that's past.
All thought is folly, every path is dark;
Truth gleaming fairly in the distant haze,
On near approach becomes the blackest lie.
Man and his soul may go, nor will I fret
To learn their mystic bonds. A worm I am,
And worm I must remain, till Death shall burst
The chrysalis, and free the web-wound wings.
Yet, oh! 'twere grand to spurn the clogging Earth,
And cleave the air towards yonder looming cloud;
To stand upon its red-bound crest and dare
The storm-king's wildest wrath.

       My thoughts
Grew dull, my eyelids slowly closed, the scene
Became confused and melted into sleep.
And far up in the blue, as yet untouched
By clouds, I saw a white descending speck.
Methought 'twas but a feather from the breast
Of some migrating swan, that Earthward fell,
And watched to see it caught upon the wind,
And sail a tiny kite to fairy land.
But circling down, the speck became a dove,
A heron, then a swan, and larger still,
Till I could mark a pair of great white wings,
Between which hung its wondrous form. Still down
It swept, till scarce above the trees it stood,
Resting on quivering wings, as if it sought

A place to 'light. I saw then what it was,
A steed of matchless beauty, agile grace,
Combined with muscled strength ; but ere I drew
The first long breath, that follows such surprise,
It gently downward swooped, and at my feet,
With dainty hoof, the turf impatient pawed.
Enrapt, I gazed upon its beauteous form,
Its sculptured head, and countenance benign,
The soft sad eyes, the arrow-pointed ears,
The scarlet nostrils opening like two flowers,
The sinewed neck, curved like a swimming swan's,
The splendid mane, a cataract of milk,
That poured its foaming torrents half to Earth,
The tap'ring limbs, tipped with pink-hued hoofs,
That touched our soil with a proud disdain ;
The dazzling satin coat, and netting veins,
And last the glorious wings, whose feathers lapped
Like scales of creamy gold. What seemed a cloth
Of woven snow, with richest silver fringe,
Draped with its gorgeous folds the shining flanks.

It was perfection's type, the absolute,
Not one defect ; the tiniest hair was smooth,
The smallest feather's edge unfrayed. The eyes
Without the slightest bloodshot fleck, or mote.
No fault the microscope could have revealed,
Though magnifying many million times.
So great my wonder, that I could not move,
But lay entranced, while he stood waiting there ;

Till wearied with my long delay, he raised
His wings half-way, and eager trembled them,
As bluebirds do when near their mate; a neigh
Of trumpet tone aroused me. Then I sprang
Upon his back, and wildly shouted " On !"
A spring with gathered feet, a clash of wings,
That made me cling in terror, and we swept
From Earth into the air. Woods, plains, and streams
Flashed by beneath, as, up and on, we charged
Straight to the frowning cloud.
                              My very brain
Reeled with our lightning speed, and dizzy height,
And oh ! how silent was the air. No sound,
Except the steady beat of fanning wings,
That hurled us on a rod at every stroke.
The bellowing winds were loosed and fiercely met
Our flight. They tossed the broad white mane across
My shrinking shoulders, like a scarf of silk ;
They blew the strong-quilled feathers all awry,
And like a banner beat the silvered cloth ;
But swerving not to right or left, we pressed
Straight onward to the goal.
                              At last I reined
My steed upon the shaggy ridge of clouds,
And caracoled along the beetling cliffs,
Up to the very summit. Then I paused.
Behind me lay the world with all its hum
Of life, the distant city's veil of smoke,
The village gleaming white amid the trees ;

The very orchard I had left, now seemed
A downy nest of green, and far away
I caught the shimmer of the sea, where sails,
With glidings, glittered like the snowy gulls.
Behind all was serene, before me seethed
The caldron of the tempest's wrath.

       Thick clouds,
Thrice tenfold blacker than the black outside
We see, deep in the crackling fire-crypts writhed,
And boiling rose and fell. A deafening blast
Roaring its thunder voice above the scene,
As if the fiends of Hell concocted there
The scalding beverage of the damned.

         My horse
Had snuffed the fumes, and rearing on the brink,
That fearful brink, an instant pawed the air,
And then sprang off. A suffocating plunge,
Through heat and blinding smoke, while to his neck
Convulsively I clung! Down through the cloud,
Until I gasped for breath, and felt my brain
Was bursting with the fervid weight.

        He stopped
Before a large pavilion, round whose walls,
As faithful guard, a whirlwind fierce revolved,
And at whose folded door, with dazzling blade,
The lightning stood a sentinel. My steed
Was passport, and I passed within, but stopped
Upon the threshold, dumb with awe. The walls
Seemed blazing mirrors, whose bright polished sides

"Threw back in flaming lineaments" the form
Of every object there,—a trembling wretch,
With pallid countenance, shown ghastly red,
Upon a horse of War's own direful hue,
I saw reflected there. The floor seemed made
Of tesselated froth, whose bubbles burst,
With constant hissing, into rainbow sparks;
While like the sulph'rous canopy, that drapes,
At evening's close, a gory battle-field,
The roof of crimson vapor drooped and rose,
With every breath and every slightest sound.
And in the centre of the glowing room,
Upon a sapphire throne an Angel sat,
Upon whose brow Rebuke and Wisdom met.
He gazed upon me with such pitying look,
And yet withal so stern, that all my pride
Was gone, and humble as a conquered child,
I ran with trembling haste and near the throne
Kneeled down.
          "Vain man," he said, "and hast thou dared
To doubt the providence of God; Behold!"
And, lo! one side of the pavilion rose,
And out before me lay Immensity.
The frothy floor, now crumbling from the edge,
Dissolved away close to my very feet,
The walls contracted their three sides in one,
And I, beside a throne I dared not grasp,
Stood on a narrow ledge of fragile foam,
That clicked its thousand little globes of air,

With every motion of my feet.
      Far down
Below, the black abyss of chaos yawned,
So vast, I gasped while gazing, and so deep,
The Sun's swift arrowy rays flash down for years,
And scarcely reach the dark confines, or fade
Amid the impenetrable gloom. Methought
'Twas Hell's wide jaws, that opened underneath
The Universe, to catch as crumbs the worlds
Condemned, and shaken from their orbit's track.
And long I looked into the vast black throat,
To trace the murky glow of hidden fire,
Or catch the distant roar. But all was still ;
No murmur broke the silence of its gloom,
No faintest glimmer told of lurking light,
No smoky volumes curdled in its depths;
As dark as Egypt's plague, serenely calm,
Defying light, the empty hall of Space,
Where twinkled not a star nor blazed a sun.—
A grand eternal night! ·
      I shuddering turned,
With freezing blood to think of falling there,
And stretched a palsied hand to touch the throne.
The Angel's eye was sterner, as he waved
Towards my steed, who seemed of marble carved.
The wings unfolded, and he leaped in air,
Beating from off the ledge the flakes of foam
That sank, with airy spirals, out of sight.
With slanting flight across the gulf he sheared ;

The moveless wings were not extended straight,
But stood, at graceful angle, o'er his back,
As, swifter than a swooping kite, he flashed
Adown the gloom. His flowing mane broad borne
Out level, like another wing; his feet
With slow ellipses moving alternate,
As if he trod an unseen path. 'Twas grand
To see his graceful form, more snowy white
Against the black relief, sublimely float
Across the dark profound, and down its depths,
Pass from my view. As when an Eagle soars
Beyond our vision in the azure sky,
We wonder what he sees, or whither flies,
So I stood wondering if he would return,
And what his destination down th' abyss.

Above, around, all was infinitude
Of light and harmony. The worlds moved on,
In mazy multitude, without a jar,
Star circling planet, planet sun, and sun;
In systems, farther yet and farther still,
Till multiplying millions mingled formed
A sheet of milky hue. And far beyond
The last pale star, appeared a dazzling spot,
That flamed with brightness so ineffable
The eye shrank 'neath its gleam. And from its light,
Athwart the endless realms of space, there streamed
A radiance that illumed the Universe,
And down across the chasm of Chaos flung

A wavering band of purple and of gold.
And in that distant spot my 'wildered eyes
Traced out the figure of a Great White Throne,
Round which, in grand and solemn majesty,
Slow swept Creation's boundless macrocosm.—
I felt too insignificant to pray,
But mutely waited for the Angel's words.
He spoke not, but the curtains closer drew,
And left a narrow opening in front.
Then with a speed the lightning ne'er attained,
Our cloud pavilion swiftly whirled through space.
A speed that would have slain me with its haste,
Had not the Angel been so near.
                                        As on the cars,
We dash through towns, and mark the hurrying
        lights,
Or shudder at an engine rattling by;
So through our door, I marked the countless worlds,
In clustering systems, chained by gravity,
Flash by in endless course. A second's time
Sufficed to pass our little group of stars,
That waltz about our Sun, as if it lit
The very Universe. Then systems came,
Round which our system moves, and these
Round others, till the series grew so vast
I shrank from looking. Great Alcyone,
Our telescopic giantess, a babe
Amid the monsters of the starry tribe,
The last familiar face in Heaven's throng,

Blazed by the door; an instant, out of sight!
And after all that we have known or named
On Earth were far behind, the millions came
In endless multitude; and on we swept,
Till worlds became a dull monotony,
And all the wonders of the Heavens were shown.
A planet wheels its huge proportions past,
Its pimpled face with red volcanoes thick,
That, with our speed, seem girdling bands of light;
A Sun, whose flame would fade our yellow spark,
Roars out a moment at our narrow door
As through its blaze we fly, then dies away,
Casting a weird and momentary gleam
Over the Angel's unrelenting face;
A meteor tears its whizzing way along,
All showering off the scintillating sparks
That mark its trail.   Far off, a comet runs
Its bended course, the mighty fan-like tail
Lit with a myriad globes of dancing fire,
That seemed like Argus' eyes on Juno's bird.
And on we sped, till one last Sun appeared,
A monstrous hemisphere of concave shape,
And brilliancy intense; it seemed to stand
On great Creation's bounds, a lense of light.
Close by its vast red rim we shaved, and passed
Beyond, to empty space unoccupied.
No world, no sun, no object passed the door;
The steady blue, tinged with a brightening gold,
Alone was seen.   Still on and on we flew,

Until a score of ages seemed elapsed,
And I had near forgotten Earth and home.

And yet the air grew brighter, till I feared
That we approached a sun, so infinite
In light, that I should sink in dazzled death.

We came to rest, the curtains fell away,
And lo! I stood within the light of Heaven.
And oh! its glorious light! No angry red,
Nor blinding white, nor sickly yellow glare,
But one vast golden flood, sublime, serene,
No object near, on which it could reflect,
It formed the very atmosphere itself,
An air in which the soul could bathe and breathe,
And ever live without its fleshly food.

No object near, for on the farthest bounds
Of space immense as mortal can conceive,
Creation hung, a group of clustering motes,
Where only suns were seen as tiny specks,
And Earth and smaller stars were out of sight.
No object near, for father than the motes,
The walls of Heaven, in glorious grandeur loomed,
Yet near as flesh and blood could bear.
                                    How grand!
From infinite to infinite extent
The glittering battlements were spread, the height
Above conception, built of purest gold,

Yet gold transparent, for I could discern
Though indistinctly, domes and spires beyond,
And all the wondrous workmanship divine,
That blazed with jewels, flashing varied hues
In perfect union ; and bright happy fields,
That bloomed with flowers immortal, in whose midst
The crystal river ran.   And through the scenes
Thronged million forms, that each sought happiness,
From million varied, purified desires.
Each face serenely bright as Evening's star,
And some I thought I knew, were dear to me ;
But as I gazed, they ever disappeared.

Along the walls, twelve gates of pearl were seen,
So great their breadth, and high their jewelled arch,
That Earth could almost trundle in untouched,
And in each arch was fixed a giant bell
Of silver, with a golden tongue that hung,
A pendant sun.   So wide the silver lips,
That Chimularee plucked up by the roots,
And as a clapper swung within its circ,
Would tinkle, like a pebble, noiselessly
Against the rigid side.   And as the saved
Were brought in teeming host, by Angel bands,
Before the gates, the bells began their swing;
And to and fro the ponderous tongue was hurled,
Till through the portals marched the shouting
       throng,
And then it fell against the bounding side.

And loud and long their booming thunder
Rends the golden air asunder,
While the ransomed, passing under,
    Fall in praise beneath the bells,
    Whose mighty throbbing welcome tells;
And the Angels hush their harps in wonder—
    Bells of Heaven, glory booming bells!

Gentler now, the silver's shiver
Purls the rippling waves that quiver
Through the ether's tide forever,
    Mellow as they left the bells,
    Whose softening vibrate welcome tells;
And the quavers play adown the river—
    Bells of Heaven, softly sobbing bells!

Then the dreamy cadence dying,
Sings as soft as zephyrs sighing;
Faintest echoes cease replying
    To the murmur of the bells,
    Whose stilling tremor welcome tells,
Faintly as the snow-flakes falling, lying—
    Bells of Heaven, dreamy murmuring bells!

And in and out those Gates of Pearl, there streamed
A ceaseless throng of Angels, errand bound.
From one came forth a band of choristers,
With shining harps, and sweeping out through space,
Their long white lines bent gracefully, they sang.

Although so far away, that purest air
Brought every note exquisite to my ear.
' Twas richly worth life's toil, to catch one bar
Of Heavenly melody. Oh! I would give
My pitiful existence, once again
To hear the strains that floated to me then,
So full, so deep, so ravishingly sweet;
Now gentle as a mother's lullaby,
They almost died away, then louder rose,
And rolled their volumes through the boundless
    realms,
That trembled with the diapason grand;
Until eternal echoes caught the strain,
And glory in the highest swelled sublime.

Entranced, I lay with 'wildered half-closed eyes,
Till from another gate, another host
Marched forth, the armies of the living God.
Beneath their thunder-tread all Heaven shook,
And at their head the tall Archangel strode.
How grandly terrible his mien! His face
Lit with a soul that only kneels to Three;
The lofty brows drawn slightly to a frown,
The eyes that beam with vast intelligence,
The depths of distance piercing with their glance;
The chiselled lips, compressed with stern resolve,
Yet marked with lines and curves of tender love,
That ever with a sigh Wrath's vial broke
Upon the doomed. His splendid form so tall,

That as he paused a moment in the gate
His dazzling crest just grazed the silver bell.
He wore no arms nor armor, save a sword
Without a sheath, that blazed as broad and bright
As sunset bars that shear the zenith's blue—
A sword, that falling flatly on the host
Of Xerxes, would have crushed them as we crush
A swarm of ants. An edge-stroke on the Earth
Would gash the rocky shell to caverned fire.
Unfolding wings would shake a continent,
He floated down the depths. Behind him came
A million foll'wers, counterparts in all,
Save presence of command.

      I wondered not
That one should breathe upon the Syrian might,
And still the sleeping hearts, four thousand score.

And from Creation's little corner came
The Guardian Angels, bearing in their arms
Their charges during life. As laden bees,
They flew to Heaven's hive; and some passed by
So closely I their burdens could discern;
And though they came from far-off, unseen Earth,
The stiffened forms were borne all tenderly.
Some bore the dimpled babe, with soft-closed eyes,
As if upon its mother's breast; its hands,
Unhardened yet by toil of life, its face
Unfurrowed yet by care's sharp plough; and some
The age-bent form, with ghostly silvered hair,

And features gaunt in death, that would have seemed
A hideous sight, in any light but Heaven's;
Some bore the rich, who made of Mammon friends,
Who wore the purple with a stainless soul;
Some bore the poor, who mastered poverty,
And broke the ashen crust beneath God's smile;
Their work-worn hands now folded peacefully,
And passing towards the harp, the weary feet,
So often blistered in life's bitter dust,
To tread with kings the golden streets of Heaven;
And some the maiden form bore lovingly,
So fair, they seemed twin sisters.
                              And I saw,
That, passing through the amber air, they caught
Its glowing dust upon them, and were changed,
The livid to the radiant.   Then as they
Approached the City, all the walls were thronged,
And all the harps were throbbing to be swept.
And mid the throng there moved a dazzling Form,
The jewels of whose crown were shaped like thorns.
He stood to welcome, and the gates unclosed,
And passing through them, all the death sealed
      eyes
Were opened, and they lived!
                              And then I knew
What happiness could mean.   To leave the Earth,
With all its torturing pains and ills of flesh;
The lingering, long disease, the wasted frame,
And, e'en in health, the constant dread of death,

That like the sword of Damocles impends,
And none may tell its fall.

                       And worse than flesh,
The tortures of the mind in fetters bound ;
Its chafings at its puling impotence,
Its longing after things beyond its reach,
Its craving after knowledge never given,
Its constant discontent with present time,
Its looking towards a future, that but breaks
To light alone in distance, never near ;
Its maddening retrospect o'er wasted life,
And loss of golden opportunities ;
Its consciousness of merit none admit,
Its sense of gross injustice from the world ;
The forced reflections on the sway of self,
And consequent contempt for all mankind,
Or shameful servitude to their regard ;
The poisoned thorns, that skirt the " Narrow Way ;"
The sneering laugh, the tongue of calumny,
The envious spites and hates 'tween man and man,
The doubts that swarm with thought about our soul,
That whispers all our labor here is vain,
That death is but extinction, Heaven a myth !

To leave all these, and find a perfect life,
To know that Heaven is sure eternally,
That sickness ne'er again will waste our frame,
That death shall never come again.   The mind
In perfect peace and happiness ; the hidden

Spread out before its ken; a sweet content
Pervading every thought, because "just now"
Yields happiness as great as future years;
Because Life's highest end is now attained.
The consciousness of merit, with reward
Surpassing far all we deserved. A Home
Of perfect peace, no envious spite or hate
Within its sacred walls, but all pure love
Towards our fellows, gratitude to God,
A gratitude that all Eternal life
Will not suffice to prove. 'T were joy enough
To lie before the Throne, and ever cry
Our thanks for mercy so supreme! And oh!
The vast tranquillity of those who feel
That life on Earth is ended, Heaven gained!

The Angel marked my gaze of rapt delight,
And said, "Wouldst thou go nearer?" Swift as light
We moved towards the City. On the steps,
In dreamy ecstasy, I lay, afraid to move,
Lest all the panorama should dissolve.
I cared not that I was unfit to go,
I cared not that I must return to Earth;
I felt one moment in the Golden walls
Was worth a dungeon's chains "threescore and ten."
The glory of its music, and its light,
Grew too intense, and sense forsook my brain.

Again my eyes unclosed, and 'mid the stars,

Familiar faces of the telescope,
We sped, while on the last confines of space,
The City lay with golden halo girt.
The systems passed, we neared old homelike Earth ;
And far enough to take a hemisphere
At single glance, we paused.   The little globe
Was puffing on, like Kepler's idea-beast,
With breath like tides, and echo sounds of life ;
Thus trundling on its journey round the sun
While o'er its back swarmed men the parasites.
As rustic lad, who visits some great town,
Returns ashamed of humble country home,
So I now blushed to own the world I'd thought
Was once so great.
            The Angel pointed down,
And said, " Behold the vast domains of Earth !
Behold the wondrous works of man, that calls
Himself the measure of the Universe !
Those gleaming threads are rivers, and the pools
His boundless oceans.   Those slow-gliding dots
The gallant ships, in which he braves the storms.
The largest white one, see, is laboring now
Beneath a cloud, your hand from here might span ;
What tiny tossings, like a jasmine's bloom
That drifts along the ripples of a brook !
Now on the wave, now 'neath it, now 'tis gone ;
The pool hath gulfed it like a flake of snow.
See, there are railroad lines, what works of art !
Thou canst not see the blackened threadlike tracks,

But thou mayst see the thundering train, that
    creeps
Across the landscape like a score of ants
Well laden, tandem, crawl across the floor.
'Twill take a day to reach yon smoky patch
Of pebbles! 'Tis a great metropolis!
Where Man is proud in power and lasting strength;
Where Art hath budded into perfect bloom,
Where towering domes defy the touch of Time,
And rock-ribbed structures reck not of his scythe.
On every side, proclaimed Creation's lord,
Poor flattered Man the title proudly takes—
One little gap of Earth, and not a spire
Would lift its gilded vane; the very dust
Would never rise above the chasm's mouth.

And mark yon crowd outside the city's bounds,
They hail Man's triumph over Nature's laws;
He conquers gravity, and dares to fly!
The speck-like globe slow rises in the air,
While all the throng below shout, "God-like Man!"
How pitiful! The flag-decked car but drags
Its way, a finger's breadth above their heads,
And falls, a few leagues off, into the sea;
When ships must rescue Man, the king of air!
"He soon will touch the stars," enthusiasts cry;
His highest flights ne'er reach the mountain-top,
That lifts its mole-hill head above the plain.

What different views above and underneath!
From one, the silken pear cleaves through the cloud,
And floats, beyond your vision, in the blue,
And franchised Man no longer wears Earth's chain ;
The other sees him drifting o'er the ground,
Beneath the level of the hills around,
The captive still of watchful gravity.

Upon yon strip of land, two insect swarms
Are drawn up, front to front, in serried lines ;
These are the armies, 'neath whose trampling tread
The very Earth doth tremble, now they join
In dreadful conflict.   From the battling ranks
Leap tiny bits of flame, and puffs of smoke,
Where thundering cannon belch their carnage forth ;
The heated missile cleaves its sparkling way,
The screaming shell its smoke-traced curve ; the sword
Gleams redly with the varnish of its blood,
The bayonets like ripples on a lake.
How palsied every arm, how still each heart!
If one discharge of Heaven's artillery roared
Above their heads—not that faint mutter thou
Perchance hast heard from some electric cloud,
But when a meteor curves immensity,
And bursts in glittering fragments that would dash
Thy world an atom from their path.   But God
Hath thrown the blanket of His atmosphere
Around the Earth, and shield, it from the jar
Of pealing salvos, that reverberate

Through Heaven's illimitable dome.

                             Yet thou,
The meanest of thy race of worms, hast dared
To question God's designs. Know then that He
Ordains that all, His glory shall work out.
The coral architect beneath the wave
Doth magnify Him, as the burning sun
That lights a thousand worlds. His power directs
The mechanism of a Universe,
Whose vastness thou hast been allowed to see,
And yet the mottled sparrow in the hedge
Falls not without His notice. Magnitude
Is not the seal of power, though man thinks so;
The least brown feather of the sparrow's wing,
In adaptation to its end displays
God's wisdom, as the ocean. Harmony
Is Heaven's watchword, key to all designs.
A tendency towards perfection's end
Pervades Creation; to this perfect end,
The polity Divine is leading Earth.
Endowed with reason, Man, perforce, is free;
And God, foreseeing how he'll freely act,
Adjusts all circumstance accordingly.
The order of this sequence, Man doth learn
In part; adapts himself to these fixed laws;
And thus is formed a general harmony.
Although the individual may oppose,
His foreseen freedom, acting in a net
Of circumstance, secures the wished-for end.

The bloodiest wars are sources of great good,
Invasive floods rouse national energies,
Or, mingling, form a greater people still;
Hume's skepticism foils its own design,
And rouses lusty champions of the Truth,
Who build its walls far stronger than before.
Poor sordid Man! like all your gold-slave race,
You deem wealth happiness. Hence, all your doubts
About God's providence are based on gold.
The wicked have it, and the righteous not.
What you assert is oftenest reversed,
And in a census of the world, you'd find
The good, in every land, the wealthiest.
But Earth is not the bar where Man is judged;
But only where free-will and circumstance
May join in general progress. Gold is good!
Then good depends on use of circumstance,
And not on moral merit. Well 'tis so!
For were the righteous only blessed, all men
Would righteousness pursue, from sordid aims,—
The most devout, who love their money best;
And thus good actions' essence would be lost,
That they be done for good, within itself,
And not for benefit to be conferred.

Then for your doubts about the righteous poor;
A certain law is fixed for general good,—
Some actions yield a gain and some a loss.
A wicked man may use the first, and gain,

A righteous man may use the last, and lose;
The wicked does not gain by wickedness,
But by compliance with this natural law.
The righteous, still as righteous, might have gained
By different course of conduct, had he known;
But his condition. now, can but be changed
By special miracle; but miracles,
In favor of the righteous, would destroy
All strife for good as good.
                          The poor may find
Their compensation in another world;
And even here, in consciousness of right,
In surety of Heav'n, and peace of mind.
And in the case you 've stated, like all those
Who talk as you have done, you over-draw,
And color more with Fancy than with Truth.
You 'll find no widow, perfect in her trust,
As you 've described, who is so destitute.
Go search the lanes and alleys; where you find
The greatest squalor, there is greatest crime;
For poverty is oftenest but a name
For reckless vice, and vile depravity.
Your case is but exception to the rule,
And not the rule, of Providence. To give
The righteous, only, wealth and worldly store
Would take away Man's freedom, and all good.

But I will answer in your folly's mode.
The justice, then, of Nature's laws you doubt,

Forgetting they are fixed for general good,
And not for individual. These laws,
In their effects, you praise as very good;
Yet, in their causes, call the most unjust.
The fertile fields, with grain for man's support,
Are nourished by a miasmatic air,
That, sickening but a few, feeds all the world.
While, were the air all pure, a few were well,
And millions starving. In the tropics, too,
The scenes you deprecate, themselves but cause
The very beauties you admire. Unjust,
You would enjoy effects without a cause.
The goods of Nature often take their rise
From what to man proves evil. For the goods,
He makes his mind to meet the evils; then
Can he complain, or think it hard to bear?

But Nature's dealings towards Man are just.
He knows that he is free, and Nature not;
If he opposes Nature's laws and falls,
Is Nature to be blamed? The widow's cot
Is frail; the laws of general good require
A storm; it comes, and shattered falls the cot.
Should God have saved it by a miracle,
Then all His people could demand the same,
And Earth would soon become the bar of God.
God may exert a special providence,
But Man may not detect it, as the rule
Invariable of life, and still be free;

For he were thus compelled to seek the good.
Then Nature, over Man, holds not a tyranny,
But keeps the perfect pandect of her laws,
And Man is free to obey them, or oppose.

Like shallow-thoughted reasoners of Earth,
You make assertions without slightest proof,
Or faintest shade of truth.   Your thesis, this:
God marks with disapproval all the good,
And blesses all the evil with His smile.
Entirely false in every case!   The good
Are ever happiest, in peace of mind,
In ease of conscience, and the hope of Heaven.
The wicked may be even rich, but wealth
And happiness are far from synonyms.
Is happiness the child of circumstance,
Or is it not the offspring of the mind?
And if the mind be tranquil and serene,
Does happiness not follow everywhere?
The cause of doubt in you, and many more,
Is that the thousands who profess the good,
Are ever mourning their unhappy lot,
And sighing o'er the gloomy, narrow way;
The tribulation of the promise read
Without its good cheer context.   These are they
Who stamp with misery's blackest seal, a life
Of righteousness.   By these you cannot judge,
For they are not what they profess, and would
Be miserable in Heaven, unless changed.

But take the truly good, one who 's content
To take whate'er befalls, submissively;
Who feels assured that all works for the best;
Take him, in all conditions, rich or poor,
In sickness or in health, in pain or ease;
Compare your happy wicked, with his gold,
'Twill not require a moment to decide
Which one is happier!

                  Again, you ask   •
Why Man was not created happy, and kept so?
His very freedom and intelligence
Prevents a forcèd happiness. The ends
Of all Creation would be marred, and Man
Lose personality. A happiness
Made universal, asks morality
That 's universally compelled; and lost
Is all the scheme of virtue and reward.
Man, forced to action, would degenerate
Into a listless, lifeless thing; the world
Lose all its fine machinery of thought
Combined with action. Beautiful variety
Could not exist, dull sameness would be life.
But Man is placed, with free intelligence,
. Amid surroundings from which he may cull
A happiness intense, whate'er their nature be.
If bright, the consciousness they are deserved;
If gloomy, sweet reflections that they drape
A future all the brighter for their gloom.

But Man, within himself, your puzzle proves;
And not to you alone, for Angel wings
Have hovered o'er your globe, and Angel minds
Peered curiously into his soul, to learn
Its mysteries, in vain.   The Mind Supreme
That formed the soul, alone can understand
Its wondrous depths.   'Tis not surprising then
That Man has tried in vain to know himself.
His mind, compared with his body, seems so great,
He deems its power unlimited.   He finds
It weak, before the barriers of thought,
That gird it, mountain high, on every side.
No path can he pursue that's infinite.
And few exist, that do not thither lead.
Hence all the vagaries that have obtained
Among your race.   The doubt of everything,
Is only too far tracing of a thought
Into absurdity intense.   If you
Deem all the world effect upon yourself,
A principle of fairness would demand
That you accord the right to other men.
The question then arises, who is he
That really does exist, and all the rest
His ideas ?   Sure your neighbor has the right
To claim the honor, just as well as you !
Hume's foolish thought, extended to its length,
Will answer not a single end of life,
And terminates in nonsense none believe.

The conflict of the mental powers defeats
Your inquiries. You cannot reconcile
The unruled circumstance, with Man's free-will.
You deem the motive free, and Man its slave ;
As if the motive, unintelligent,
Could have a freedom, or a slavery !
You make the motive to exist within the mind,
When it, perforce, must be without. You get
The unruled motive from the circumstance,
When this itself must act upon the mind,
And if *free* motives rise within the mind,
They are a *part*, and therefore *mind* is free.
And what you deemed a motive to the mind,
Was mental action, and its modes of thought.
The motive is confined to circumstance,
And mind the circumstance can oft control,
And even when it cannot, acts at will.

The mind may to a kingdom be compared,
Where Reason occupies the throne. Beneath
Its sceptre bow, in perfect vassalage,
The faculties, desires, and appetites.
These then are acted on by motive powers,
And straight report the action to their king,
Who does impartially decide for each.
The unruled motive is without the mind,
And forms no part of it, although the parts,
Receiving motive action, so are called.
Thus when you hunger, the desire of food,

Confined to mind, is not a motive power;
But urged by motive bodily demand,
It tells the need to Reason, who decides.
Thus when you pare your peach, the tempting fruit
And fleshly need, move on the appetite,
Who begs the Reason for consent to eat;
Your friend's opinion of your self-control,
Is motive to Desire of esteem,
Who begs the Reason to refuse consent.
The Reason, then, like righteous judge, decrees
In favor of that one, more strongly shown;
And feels a perfect freedom in its choice.

'Tis most unfair to wait the action's end,
Then cry, the mind was forced to choose this act;
But choice is Reason's free decree. Sometimes
The Reason errs, and evil then ensues;
But Reason, now more conscious that 'tis free,
Regrets it had not acted otherwise.
By knowing what your reason deems the best,
You judge how other men will act.   You learn,
By intercourse, what they permit to change
The Reason's sentence.   So, while with a friend,
You show your wealth, because you know he's free,
And can, and will, resist impulse to crime.
Were he not free, you'd dare not go alone
With him, for, any moment, might arise
A motive irresistible, and he
Would kill and rob, because that motive's slave.

Were he not free, you were no more secure,
In pleasant parlance, that on desert isle.

The laws are made for man, alone, as free.
For, otherwise, the motives they present
Were blind attempts to coincide with Fate.
They would complete the gross absurdity,
Of Man collective governing himself,
And therefore free, while individuals
Are helpless slaves of motives they but aid
To furnish.
       Fate, as held in fullest form,
Yourself has proved the theory of fools;
For were it true, a blind passivity
Were Man's perfection on the Earth.   Compare
The two; Free-will as held, whate'er their faith,
By every one, in daily practices;
A world of harmony, for very wars
Yield good; a mechanism complicate,
That even Angels, wondering at, admire;
A world, whose wondrous progress is maintained
By practical belief in liberty.
And on the other hand, behold a world
Of universal inactivity!
Its millions starving for delinquent Fate;—
I doubt your faith would last till dinner-time,
A morning's lapse would change a hungry globe
To firm belief in free-will work for food.

With many, God's foreknowledge binds free-will;
He knows the future, how each man will act,
And man can never change from what God knows.
They reason thus, that prescience is decree,
And what God knows will happen, must take place.
That God may know the future of *free*-will
I prove by this. Suppose two worlds alike,
And governed by two Gods. Each one can see,
And foresee all transpires in both the worlds,
Yet each o'er th' other's world exerts no power.
A man in one does wrong; the other God
May have foreseen the action for an age,
Yet had not slightest power to cause or stop.
Does his foreknowledge qualify the act?
If thus you can suppose, why not believe,
When errors flow from opposite belief?
God in the future stands, and waits for man,
Who works the present, only gift of Time.
There is no future save in God's own mind.
Man's future means continued present time;
God's future is but present time to Him,
In which He lives, not will live when it comes.
Man's acts He sees as done, not to be done.
And God compels not more than Man does Man,
Who sees his fellow's deeds, not causes them.
Man only knows Man's present acts; but God
The future sees, as present to His mind.

To end with perfect proof, you know you 're free.

This all the world attests, and each believes.
How subtle soe'er may his reasoning be,
He contradicts it throughout all his life;
And all his plans, and all the right and wrong
Of self and friends he bases on free-will.
If disbelief no inconvenience prove,
Few men believe what is not understood;
And yet the most familiar things of life
Are far beyond their comprehension's power.
Who understands the turning of the food
To sinew, muscle, blood, and bone? yet who
Will starve because he knows not how 'tis done?
Who understands the mystery of birth,
And when and where the soul originates?
And yet a million mothers bend, to-day,
O'er tender babes, and know that they exist;
A billion people know they once were born.
Who understands the mystery of death,
And how the soul is severed from its clay?
Yet who has not wept o'er departed ones,
Received the dying clasp, the dying look,
And known, full well, Death's bitter, bitter truth?
None comprehends the movement of a limb,
Yet many boast the powers of their's might.
Then why doubt freedom of the will, when life,
In every phase, but proves its certain truth?
The edifice of shallow theorists
Before the sweeping blade of practice falls.

Your dive into the heart yields folly's fruit;
The selfish theory, carried to its end,
Makes wrong of right, and overturns the world.
And strong it is in seeming; for the self,
In human conduct, plays important part.
But 'tis not action's only source, nor dims
The quality of every action's worth.
'Tis true that Man exists in self alone,
And in himself feels pain or pleasure.   True,
An instinct teaches to avoid the one,
And seek the other; true, that every act,
How small soe'er, gives pleasure or gives pain.
Yet thousand deeds are done without regard
To one or other, or effect on Self.
Howe'er an action may affect the Self,
If he that acts has not a thought of it,
The action is not selfish.   You appeal
To Man, and so will I appeal to you.
You find a helpless brute, with broken limb,
Upon the roadside, moaning out its pain.
Now, though to aid will surely pleasure give,
And to neglect will cause remorseful pain,
Is there a single thought of this, when you,
With kindest hand, bind up the swollen bruise,
And hold the grateful water to its mouth?
Is not each thought to ease the sufferer's pain?
Is not the Self first found, when on your way
You go, with lighter heart, for kindness done?
And while you think with pleasure on the deed,

Would you not feel despised in your own eyes,
If consciousness revealed 'twas done for Self?
But should you say that Self was thus concealed,
And still evoked the deed, the argument
The same; if Self was out of thought, the deed
Had other source.

        In all, you thus mistake
The deed's effect, unthought of, for its source.
God, in His wisdom, hath affixed to good
Performed, a pleasure, and to evil, pain.
But selfish actions are not good, you 've said,
And therefore cannot slightest pleasure yield.
Here, then, your system contradicts itself;
All actions emanate from love of Self,
To find the highest pleasure for that Self;
And yet the pleasure 's lost by very search;
What good soe'er apparently is sought,
The consciousness of selfish aims destroys.
And here is wisdom manifest. When Self
Would seek the good, for pleasure to the Self,
The pleasure is not found; but when it seeks
The good alone, true pleasure is conferred.
I mean the Self of soul, not Self of flesh;
For pleasure to the sense, to be attained
Is sought; these two are mingled intricate
(And hard to separate), in thousand ways.
But when Man's higher Self would seek its good,
It must forget the Self. In every case
You instanced, Self of soul must be unthought,

For pleasure will not come at call of Self.
Your gambler none will doubt has selfish ends;
Not so the preacher, for his pleasure sought,
Would ne'er be found; it must be out of thought.
His burning eloquence, his pastoral care,
Can not proceed from any love of Self,
For Self would suffer, when it knew their source;
But as he acts from love of good, as good,
The Self is happy.   When he ascertains
That some have died in sin through his neglect,
The Self is grieved, not that it was uncared,
For care of Self would not allay the pain,
But that a duty had not been performed;
That good had been neglected, as a good.
The gambler's object may be highest good
For Self, according to his estimate;
The preacher seeks a good, but not for Self;
When Self appears, the good to evil turns.
Nor is the mystic selfish in his cave,
Save that he buries talents in himself,
That might avail for good to other men;
But all his mind is bent on pleasing God,
His only thought of Self is for its pain;
And this he deems acceptable to Heaven.
You can not judge by your analysis,
But by what passes in the actor's mind.
One surely then could not be selfish termed,
Who only lived to mortify the Self,
Howe'er mistaken may his conduct be.

Nor is the man, who gives his wealth away,
If from right principles he gives. 'Tis true,
He finds a pleasure in the deed when done,
But if to gain that pleasure he has given,
It turns to gall and wormwood in his grasp.
If two men matches light, and know full well,
If one is dropped, a house will be consumed,
He is the most guilty that allows its fall.
The miser, then, who knows he does a wrong,
Is by that knowledge rendered criminal.
"The quality of actions must be judged"
From their intents, that often differ wide;
The man who shoots his friend by accident
Has no intent, and therefore does no wrong;
But he who murders does a score of wrongs,—
A score of basest motives prompt the deed,
All centred in the Self. The Christian's work
Must, from its very nature, have no Self,
Or it becomes unchristian. Man can judge,
Not from effect, but motives ascertained
By inference, and experience. The law
Is formed hereon, and modified by years.
Time teaches men that punishment will stop,
And only punishment, the spread of crime.
Instinct and Nature's order teaches you
That pain must follow wrong. A man commits
A crime; if left unpunished, he repeats;
And others, seeing his security,
Will do as he has done. So all mankind

Would hasten on to lawlessness and ruin.
But law, for real wrong inflicts a wrong,
Which would be just, did it no farther go ;
But it is proved expedient, inasmuch
As it prevents continued crime.   Then death
By law can not be murder termed, since good
In aim and end, without malicious thought.
Thus good to many flows from wrong to one
(If that may wrong be termed that takes the
        rights
By conduct forfeited), who should receive,
Though none reaped benefit.   For many's good,
The law is made, yet never does a wrong
To individuals, unless deserved.

Throughout your reas'ning, like all Earthly minds,
When dataless, essaying hidden truths,
You wander blindly in conjecture's field,
And if you find the truth, it is a chance.
You fain would raise a stone of skepticism,
By granting souls immortal unto beasts ;
You prove your pointer must possess a soul,
And by your argument, the trees have souls ;
For when an oak has fallen, every twig
May still be there, and something, life, be gone.
A chair, a table, anything you see,
Possesses something, not of any parts,
But that to which the parts are said, belong,
Then, one by one, take all the parts away,

The something called the table must exist,
For 'twas not in a part, nor is removed.

The mind of beasts exists but through their flesh,
And is developed subject to its laws,
And flesh is the condition of their life.
When flesh dissolves, the mind disintegrates,
And ceases to exist. Man feels within,
The consciousness of soul, that would survive
Though flesh were torn to shreds upon the wheel.
The parts of soul that live alone through flesh,
Must perish with it in the hour of death.

But having postulated Self, as source
Of human conduct, you compel the acts
To fit your theory. You change effect
For cause. Where'er a moral pleasure's found,
You judge that for its gain the deed was done ;
As if the pleasure could be gained by search !
That Self does enter largely into inner life
Is very plain, for everything affects,
In some way, Self ; but does the mind regard
Effect, or is its object something else ?
The appetites, affections, and desires,
You make of selfish origin, yet know
That is not selfish, which alone affects ;
But acting with a reference to effect.
The appetites are instincts ; as you breathe,
You hunger, thirst, in helplessness. Not Self,

But food or drink, the object of your thought.
And even while the taste is in your mouth,
The mind dwells on the taste, not on the Self.
Desires are partly selfish in their mode ;
Desire of knowledge, seeking honor's meed,
Is selfish ; led by curiosity,
'Tis not more selfish than an appetite.
Desire of power, esteem, and wide-spread fame,
Is selfish, when the thought of their effect
On Self shapes out the conduct; when desired
For their own sake, unselfish.
       On the list
Affections terminate, you falsely rail
The mother, and the lover ; both sincere,
And both without a thought of selfish aim.
'Tis no reproach to say the mother's love,
In fervid instinct, and development,
Is like the cow's, that God in wisdom gives.
No love so pure as that which moves the cow
To hover round her young, to bear the blows
Impatient hunger deals the udder drained,
To smooth with loving tongue the tender coat,
Or meet the playful forehead with her own ;
With threatening horn, to guard approach of harm ;
And watch, with ceaseless care, the charge in sleep.
Her careful love continues, till the calf
Has grown beyond her need, and ceases then.
A mother loves because it is her child :
This is the surest reason you could give.

Th' affection is spontaneous in her breast,
But fed and strengthened by his life, if good.
The opposites to love you named, affect
Her love, by not an injury done to Self,
But by their evil, which her soul abhors.
Her son's antagonism 's not to her,
But to the good she loves. Her heart withdraws
Its twining tendrils from unworthiness.
As usual, you select supposed effects,
And then assume their causes. Could you see
The mother's heart, you 'd find the loss of love
Caused not by wrong to her, but wrong abstract,
Developed in the concrete deeds of crime.
Her love is governed by a moral sense,
Or idea of the good; the people's thought
About herself comes in as after-part.
Bad treatment to herself, although it pain,
Deals not a fatal blow to love, except
As showing lack of principle in him.
And so your lover is not hurt in Self,
But moral sense. The loved one's perfidy,
And not her ridicule, beheads your love ;
Her stunning words were playful pleasantry,
Did they not show the baseness of her heart.
Indeed, to turn your reasoning on yourself,
Her manner even towards you has not changed,
And were you present, she would still seem yours ;
Her eaves-dropped words do not affect the Self,
Save as they show her falsity of heart.

And tossing on your pillow, through the night,
The crushing thought of wrecked integrity
Gives deeper pain than all her ridicule.
And Self, though pained at thought of being
    duped,
Enjoys relief in thought of its escape.
To show that Love is built on higher grounds
Than paltry good for Self; that it must have,
As corner-stone, a percept of the good,
Existing in the object loved, suppose
You 're on the topmost height of wildest love,
Your arm around her, and your lingering kiss
Upon her lips; and Self is king of love.
She, nestling on your shoulder, finds 'tis wrong,
That love, however true, may grow too warm;
That every kiss, however pure, abstracts
Some little part from maiden modesty,
And steals a pebble from her honor's wall,
And rising with the firm resolve, says, " Cease,
Unwind your arm, restrain your fervid lips;
It may be wrong, and right is surely safe ! "
Now though the Self is bitterly denied,
The rapturous clasp and tender kiss forbid,
Is not your love increased a thousand-fold ?
Do not you feel intensely gratified
At this assurance of her moral worth ?
And would you, for the world, breathe aught to
    cause
Her pain, or least regret for her resolve ?

How firm your trust, how sweet your confidence!
You know 'twas not capricious prudery,
For your caresses had been oft received;
Nor was it sly hypocrisy to win
Your heart, for that was long since hers. No
    thought,
But spotless purity, inspired the act;
And you are happy, though the Self's denied.

The little things of life, that men account
Without a moral value, may be done
With reference to Self; but oftenest,
The mind regards the act, not its effect
Upon the Self. The code of Etiquette,
The small amenities of social life,
The converse, and the articles of dress,
May all belong to Self; but moral acts,
Those known as right or wrong, have higher source
Than Self in any mode.
              Within Man's breast
There's something, apprehending good and bad,
Called conscience, or the moral sense; it views,
Impartially, each act of his, decides
Its quality by rule of right and wrong;
All trust its judgments most implicitly.—
The good is found, yields greatest happiness;
Yet seek it for the sake of happiness,
And good is evil, with its misery!
The good must be pursued, because a good,

The evil shunned, because an evil. Thus,
The moral sense discerns these qualities
In others, and directs our love.
                  A blow
The deadliest to our love, would be a blow
Aimed at the principle of good. A love,
Existing through the injuries done to Self,
May meet the public's praise, and feel its own ;
But love would merit self-contempt, that loved
Whate'er opposed the good. The son may treat
The mother with unkindness, yet her love
Be undiminished ; if he lie, or steal,
Her love is less ; she cannot love his deed,
And cannot love the heart from which they flow.
So with the youth who gives his chair to Age,
He does not so resent that Self's denied
Its meed of thanks, as that ingratitude
Should thus be manifest, in little things.
A comrade, served the same, would anger cause.

But him who would give up the highest Self,
The soul, for others' good, you deem a fool;
And ask why sacrifice ne'er claimed a soul ?
Because the soul cannot be sacrificed ;
No harm to that can others benefit.
But if it could, how truly grand the man
Who 'd take eternal woe for fellow-men !
But God, who makes the soul the care of life,
Makes every soul stand for itself alone,

And in His wisdom hath ordained this law :
The greater good man gets for his own soul,
The greater good on others' he confers,
While evil to himself, an evil gives.

Then comes the question of this abstract good,
That moral sense declares the end of life.
What is its nature ? whence does it arise ?
And whence does man derive the half-formed
    thought?
You have compared the systems that define,
Each in its way, the hidden theory.
None satisfy, though each some element
Sets forth in clear distinctness.   Take them all,
Select the true of each, as Cousin does,
And will eclecticism satisfy ?
And does the soul not cry for something more ?
For something that it feels 'twill never reach,
The good, as known to minds unclogged with flesh ?
Man takes the dim outlines of abstract thought,
And seeking to evolve their perfect form.
The very outlines grow more indistinct ;
As gazing at a star will make it fade.
Man's only forms of good are blent with flesh,
And when he seeks to take the flesh away,
And leave the abstract, he is thus confused,
As if he should withdraw the wick and oil,
And seek to find the flame still in the lamp.

To learn the source of ideas of the Good,
Trace Man collective, to his babyhood;
For 'mid the prejudice of full-grown thought,
The truth would be effectually concealed.
Through every people scattered o'er the globe,
There does prevail some idea of a God;
Though rude and barbarous this idea be,
It still, in some form, does exist.   The good,
With all, bears reference to this thought;
And what this Deity approves is good,
And what He disapproves is bad.   Men learn
What He approves, and what He disapproves,
By revelation, inference, and instinct.
God's sanction then is origin of Good,
Though afterwards men learn the sweet effects,
And practise it for its own sake; and call
Their little effort, grandest abstract truth.
Developing in intellectual strength,
They plaster up this good in various forms,
Until, refined beyond all subtilty,
It seems to them a self-existent good.

The good is then a certain quality,
In actions, or existence, that assures
Divine approval.   This vast idea, God,
Creation sows in every human heart;
All Nature's grand designs demand a God,
A God intelligent.   The same instinct
That tells His being, teaches what He loves;

And what He loves with every people's good.
But diff'rent nations entertain ideas
Diverse in reference to a Deity,
And different notions of what pleases Him.
One deems the care of God's child-gift her good ;
Another tears the heart-strings from her babe,
And feeds, for good, the sacred crocodile.

The good lies in the thought of pleasing God :
The consciousness that God is pleased with us,
A pleasure yields, and good might there be sought
For pleasure's sake, and prove a selfish aim ;
But moral selfishness a pain imparts,
And good, for pleasure sought, defeats the search.

The good is sought because it pleases God,
Not with the doer, but with what is done.
Good has its origin in th' idea God,
And what He loves ; but to continue good
It must retain approval in the act,
And not transfer it to the agent's self.
The consciousness that God approves a deed,
Makes Man approve, and thus his mind is brought
In correlation with the Mind Divine.
The man who does an alms, if done to gain
God's favor for himself, feels selfish pain ;
But if because the act, not he, will please,
He finds the pleasure. Man, as time rolls on,
Finds general laws that please or displease God,

And ranging, under these, subordinates
Amenable to them and not to God,
The moral quality of lesser deeds
He reckons by these laws, nor does ascend
To God, that gives their moral quality.
Jouffroy, in Order, placed the Abstract Good,
And paused a step below the real truth,
The idea God, whence Order emanates.

Thus Man, progressing, good withdraws from God,
And seems an independent entity,
And man denominates it, Abstract Good.
He can attain the Abstract but in part;
When mind is freed from flesh, he may attain
To its full grandeur.   Here, at most, he grasps
A faint outline, and fits it on concrete.
No concept occupies one act of mind,
But opening the lettered label, he
May count the attributes, and by an act
Complex, of memory and cognition, gain
Some idea of his Abstract.   Thus of " Man,"
One act can only cognize M-A-N,
But opening, he finds the attributes,
As " mammal," " biped," " vertebrate."   This act
Is complex, and he cannot unitize,
Save by the bundle of a word.   You 've said
It answers all the purposes of life,
Then why seek more ?. lest speculation vain
Point out dim realms, where Man can never tread,

These baffling thoughts are given, as peacocks' feet,
To Man's fond pride. The simplest avenue
Of thought, pursued, will reach absurdity,
To comprehension finite.
     Even the truth
Of numbers you presume to doubt. Two balls,
You claim, can ne'er be two unless alike.
You mingle quantity and number, foolishly,
As if a ball the size of Earth, and one,
A tiny mustard-seed, would not be two!
You deem all Mathematics wide at fault,
Because Man's powers to illustrate are weak.
Earth has oft seen a pure right angle drawn,
Because Man's sight could not detect a flaw;
And if to his discernment perfect made,
He must admit its perfect form. If life,
In every intricate demand, finds truth,
Why seek to overturn by sophistry?
You see and know Achilles far beyond
The tortoise, yet the super-wise must prove
That he can never pass the creeping thing,
Although his speed a hundred times as swift!
When Man commences, he may find a doubt
In everything; his life, his neighbor's life,
The outside world, may all be but a myth;
Then let him so believe, but let him act
Consistently; but does the skeptic so?
He crams all Nature in his little mind,
Yet how he cringes to her slightest law!

He flees the rain, and wards the cold, or fears
The lightning's glittering blow. He doubts his
  frame
Can work by mechanism so absurd,
Yet will not for a day refrain from food!

When Man compares his body and his mind,
And tries the power of each, he magnifies
The mind to Deity, and yet how small
Compared with what it has to learn! The more
Man knows, the more he finds he does not know;
And as a traveller toiling up the hill,
Each upward step reveals a wider view
Of fields of thought sublime he dares not hope
To ever reach in life; and wearily he sits
Him down upon the mountain-side, so far
Beneath its untrod top, and recklessly
Doubts everything, because beyond his grasp.

All skeptic reasoning ends, as did your own,
No fruit but blind bewilderment of thought!
And none but fools will e'er believe sincere
The faith that doubts alone by theory,
And yet approves by practice. Such is yours;
The stern necessities of life demand
A practical belief, and such is given;
And still, forsooth, because your narrow mind
Cannot contain the Truth in perfect form,
You dare deny it does exist. But few

Of skeptic minds are let to live on Earth,
And even these made instruments of good,
In calling forth defenders of the Truth,
Who add their strength to its Eternal Walls.
Then here behold God's wisdom manifest!
Amid the care of countless greater orbs,
He watches Earth, and knows its smallest thing.
While Man, as individual, is free,
Collective Man is being surely led
Towards an end, but when it will be reached,
God knows alone. Then Man will be removed
Into a higher or a lower sphere,
As he has worthy proved. With Man 'twill be
A great event; his awful Judgment-day!
When from those far-off realms, the Son shall come
With Angel retinue, and through the worlds,
Shall lead their solemn flight, to where we stand;
And as the trump shall peal its clarion tones,
And beat away Earth's gauze of atmosphere,
The millions living, and the billions dead,
Will leave the sod, and " caught up in the air,"
Shall stand before the Throne, to hear their doom.
Then, faces pale with fear, and trembling limbs,
Will be on every side, as on the air
They rest, with nothing solid 'neath their feet;
And see dismantled Earth burst into flames,
And reel along its track, a globe of fire,
The volumed smoke, a dusky envelope;
Its revolutions wrapping pliant flames,

In scarlet girdles, round its bulging waist,
And hurling streams of centrifugal sparks,
In broad red tangents, from the burning orb.
Upon the conflagration Man will gaze,
With shuddering horror; 'tis his only home,
The scene of all his fame, the source of wealth,
For which he toiled so wearily. All gone!
He would not touch a mountain of pure gold,
For 'twould be useless now! Poor, pauper Man,
Without his money, chiefest aim of life,
Stands homeless 'mid a Universe, to learn
If God will be his Father, or his Foe!
And from the blackness underneath, the swarms
Of Evil ones are thronged, their hideous forms
Half shown in lurid light, as here and there
They flit, like sharks, expectant of their prey.
Then comes the closing scene. The sentence passed,
The righteous breaking forth to joyous praise,
Shall thread Creation's wondrous maze of life,
And with their Leader, sweep towards yon Heaven;
While down the black abyss, with cries of woe
That make the darkness tremble, the condemned
Are dragged, into its gloom,—and all is o'er—
Earth's ashes float in scattered clouds through
    space—
To Man the grandest era of all Time,
To God, completion of Salvation's scheme!

But Man deems Judgment too far off for thought,

Nor will prepare for such a distant fate ;
Yet there is something, far more sure than aught
Uncertain life can offer ; its decision, too,
Is just as final as the Judgment doom ;
And still 'tis oftenest farthest from the thought.
'Tis Death, the welcome or unwelcome guest
Of every man, and yet how few prepare
For its approach ! They give all else a care ;
Wealth, honor, fame, get all their time,
While certain Death 's forgotten, till disease
Gives warning ; then with hasty penitence,
The knees are worn, the heart's thick rubbish cleared;
But oft too late ; the heart will not be cleared,
The stubborn knees will not consent to bend,
The house is set in order, while the guest,
In sable robes, stands at the throbbing door.

And now to close thy lesson, look through this !"
He gave to me a strangely fashioned glass,
Through which, when I had looked to Earth, I saw
A long black wall, that towered immensely high,
So none might see beyond. Before its length,
Mankind were ranged, all weaving busily ;
The young and old, the maiden and the man ;
The infant hands unconscious plied the thread,
The aged with a feeble, listless move.
   They wove the warp of Life, and drew its thread
From o'er the wall ; none knew how far its end
Was off, nor when 'twould reach the busy hand,

Nor did they care, in aught by action shown,
But bending o'er their work, without a glance
Towards the thread, that still so smoothly ran,
They threw the shuttle back and forth again,
Till suddenly the ravelled end appeared,
Fell from the wall, and to the shuttle crept;
And then the weaver laid his work aside,
With folded hands, was wrapped within his warp,
To wait the Master's sentence on his task.
I saw the thread, in passing through their hands,
Received the various colors, from their touch,
And tinged the different patterns that they wove.
And oh! how different in design! Some wove
A spotless fabric, whose pure simple plan
Was always ready for the ending thread;
Come when it would, no part was incomplete;
But what was done, could bear th' Inspector's eye.
And others wore a dark and dingy rag,
That bore no pattern, save its filthiness;
Fit garment for the fool who weaves for flames!
Some wove the great red woof of war,
With clashing swords, and crossing bayonets,
With ghastly bones, and famished widows' homes,
With all the grim machinery of Death,
To gain a paltry crown, or curule chair;
Perchance, before the crown or chair is reached,
The thread gives out, the work is incomplete,
And in the gory cloak his hands have wrought,
With all its stains unwashed, the hero sleeps.

Some shuttles shape the gilded temple, Fame,
And count on thread to weave its topmost dome;
But ere the lowest pinnacle is touched,
The brittle filament is snapped. Some weave
The bema, with its loud applause; and some
The gaudy chaplet of the bacchanal,
And others sweated bays of honest toil.
But all the fabrics bear the yellow stain
Of gold, o'er which the sinner and the saint
Unseemly strive, and he seems happiest
Whose work is yellowest.
      Along the wall,
" A fountain filled with blood," plays constantly,
Where man may cleanse the fabric as he weaves;
Yet few avail themselves; the waters flow,
While Man works on, without regard to stains,
Till thread worn thin arouses him to fear,
Or breaks before the damning dyes are cleansed.

And down the line I ran my anxious eyes,
To find a weaver I might recognize,
And saw, at last, a form by mirrors known.
Oh! 'twas a shameful texture that I wove,
So dark its hue, so little saving white,
Such seldom bathing in the fountain stream,
I could not look, but bowed my blushing face,
And like the publican of old, cried out,
" Be merciful to me a sinner!"
        " Rise!"

The Angel said, "and worship God alone,
Return to Earth, enjoy an humble faith,
Whose simple trust shall make thee happier
Than all the grandeur of philosophy.
Should doubts arise, remember, God's designs
Above a finite comprehension stand,
And finite doubts, about the Infinite,
Assume absurdity's intensest form.
Man, from the stand-point of the Present, looks,
And disappointed, bitterly complains
Of what would move his deepest gratitude,
Could he the issue of the morrow know.
God sees the future, and in kindness deals
To every man his complement of good.
    Remember then the weakness of thy mind,
Nor doubt because thou canst not understand.
    To gather scattered jewels thou must kneel;
So on thy knees seek truth, and thou shalt find;
The nearer Earth thy face, the nearer Heaven
Thy heart.   And now farewell!"
                              I sprang to clasp
His hand in gratitude, but with a wave
Of parting benediction, he was gone!
Then in an instant, like an aerolite,
With naught to bear me up, I fell to Earth,
Swifter and swifter, with increasing speed!
Now bursting through a sunlit bank of cloud,
And clutching, vainly, at the yielding mist,
Or through a cradling storm, with thunder charged,

Down through the open air, whose parted breath
Hissed death into my ears, while all below
Seemed rushing up to meet and mangle me.
I shrieked aloud, "Oh save me!"—

                    And awoke.

The day was o'er, and night had drawn her shades;
The twinkling eyes of Heaven shone through the
      leaves,
And lit the tiny rain-globes on the grass;
The cloud had passed, and on th' horizon's verge,
A monster firefly, with shimmering flash,
It slowly crawled behind the curve of earth.
And evening's silence deeper seemed than noon's,
For not a sound disturbed the hush of night,
Save katydids, with quavering monotones,
Returning contradictions from the trees.
All drenched and chilled, with trembling limbs I
      rose,
And homeward bent my steps; and pondering
Upon my dream, this moral from it drew:
Man cannot judge the Eternal Mind by his,
But must accept the mysteries of Life,
As purposes Divine, with perfect ends.
And in our darkest clouds, God's Angels stand,
To work Man's present and eternal good.

FINIS.